ANY WITCH WAY BUT GOODE

(UN)LUCKY VALLEY BOOK TWO

MICHELLE M. PILLOW®

CLICK HERE TO JOIN MICHELLE'S MAILING LIST

ABOUT ANY WITCH WAY BUT GOODE

WELCOME TO LUCKY VALLEY, WHERE NOTHING IS QUITE WHAT IT SEEMS.

From NY Times & USA TODAY Bestselling Author, Michelle M. Pillow, a Cozy Mystery Paranormal Romantic Comedy.

The Garden Gnome Bed and Breakfast might be a new kooky weekend getaway spot, but for Lily Goode the inheritance represents the promise of a stable future for her and her siblings. Unfortunately, the house isn't the only thing she inherited. The bed-and-breakfast also comes equipped with witchy Aunt Polly, trouble-some garden gnomes, a town that hates her, newfound magical powers that misfire, and a werewolf boyfriend she shouldn't have asked to move in with her.

When a guest is found dead during her grand

opening, Lily knows she has to solve the mystery of what happened before the B&B is closed forever.

Lucky for her, Aunt Polly is here to help save the day.

(UN)LUCKY VALLEY SERIES

Better Haunts and Garden Gnomes
Any Witch Way But Goode
More Books Coming Soon

AUTHOR UPDATES

To stay informed about when a new book in the series installments is released, sign up for updates:

michellepillow.com/author-updates

To the most amazing Bailey.

To John for putting up with author insanity.

CHAPTER ONE

LUCKY VALLEY, COLORADO

FOREVER WAS A REALLY freaking long time and looking longer by the day.

Nolan Dawson and a happily ever after might be all Lily Goode could ever want in life, but that didn't mean she was capable of having it. There was a fear inside of her, a whisper that warned her not to get too attached. She expected him to come to his senses and change his mind at any moment, and each new day added onto their future made it all the more likely that he would.

She'd known the man, what? All of three weeks before she'd invited him to move in with her on a post-magic-using high. And if that wasn't enough, she'd partnered with him in business. To an independent woman that had to look a little desperate—*move in with me, work with me, be with me every second of the day.*

What she'd initially thought was going to be a romantic ride off into the sunset had turned into a straight shot of cold, hard reality. Their life together was filled with stresses. There were days that Lily had about all the reality she could take.

And who said I love you to a man after three weeks? Surely that was too soon, too easy. She normally wouldn't say that after three years—not that any of her relationships ever lasted that long. Lily wasn't an I-love-you kind of gal. She had her reasons for being that way.

What if his feelings for her were a spell she unintentionally cast on him? What would happen when it wore off? She had to be ready for that level of heartbreak. She couldn't fall apart, not now, not with so much riding on her shoulders

Fear of being abandoned made her question if this life is the one she deserved. She hated that her mind tried to find reasons as to why she might end it first.

Nolan was a werewolf who was always *there*. Always. He never left. She supposed that is what living together meant, but he still had his own house in town. Would he go back there when he became sick of her?

Well, fine, he never left *except* to chain himself

in his old basement during a full moon, when he became a vicious, uncontrollable creature who would eat anyone who crossed his path. Talk about some serious man-period side effects.

But it wasn't just self-doubt over her relationship with Nolan that caused her stress levels to skyrocket.

It would seem Lily was full of questionable decisions. For that, she blamed her dead mother. The reemergence of Marigold Crawford in the form of a surprise inheritance had thrown Lily's entire life off track. All those childhood fears and emotions that she'd thought she'd grown out of reared their ugly heads.

Jesse, the sister Lily had known her whole life, refused to come to Colorado to accept her part of their birthright out of protest of their dead, neglectful mother. Apparently, Marigold (aka Mom) left her a safe-deposit box that only Jesse could open. No one knew what was inside. Jesse didn't seem to care.

Mara, the sister no one had known existed until a few months ago, was living with her in the house Lily had inherited from the aforementioned mother. The sanity with that sibling was questionable, and Lily was pretty sure Mara was a habitual liar. Though, to be fair, the girl had been born and raised in a barn.

Then there was Aunt Polly, who was a few almonds short of a fruitcake, and who kept trying to redecorate the house in super-feminine floral prints and doilies. Polly also had the largest collection of creepy-ass gnome statues known to man. Every time Lily turned around there was another one popping up somewhere. Her home was literally a garden gnome sanctuary.

When she had stepped out of the shower that morning, she'd found two of the creepers on the bathroom floor—one holding a flower, another with a sign that read "thanks" (Lily did *not* want to know what that referred to)—and a third sitting on a miniature toilet. He and his throne had been on the bathroom sink. There was no clue as to how they got there.

Even now, she found herself staring at a garden gnome standing by the front door, with its annoyingly cheerful face and chubby cheeks painted with too much pink. Not once had she seen them move, but sometimes when she glanced away and then back, they were no longer in the same place.

Add to all of this craziness the fact that Lily's moody brother, Dante, also lived with her. That in itself was fine. She'd lived with Dante and Jesse all of their lives. But now Dante had a pet raccoon (Polly called it a familiar) named

4

Bartholomew, who they couldn't keep out of the house. The animal kept finding his way back inside.

But wait, there's more. Much more.

She was pretty sure someone had been stealing from the guests during Garden Gnome Bed-and-Breakfast's opening week. Already three shiny trinkets were missing.

During all of these chaotic life changes, Lily had found out she was a witch. With powers and everything—misfiring, bad-luck-inducing, wayward, haphazard, shooting-out-of-the-tips-of-her-fingers, unwanted superpowers. One bad sneeze could send her teleporting through the Colorado wilderness (and it had).

The steady *whoomp-whoomp-whoomp* of a nail gun meant progress was being made on the repairs outside. That definitely went into the plus column of her relationship with Nolan. He was handy with power tools. No other contractor in a fifty-mile radius would touch anything on the Goode Estate. Her ancestors weren't remembered fondly in the area.

The estate included the Victorian house, a couple of cottages, and an old barn. Mara had burned the barn to the ground. Lily couldn't say she blamed the woman, considering their mother had kept Mara locked away inside it like an animal for years. If she behaved, she was some-times allowed into the house. Marigold had always feared that Mara's supernatural father's powers had cursed the youngest sibling and the world needed to be protected from her. Because of that, Mara had a lot of unresolved issues, and who could blame her? Marigold had been insane.

The Victorian was halfway between the haunted ghost town of Old Lucky Valley (nick-named Unlucky Valley) and a town-town called Lucky Valley. Lily owned Unlucky Valley, because why not inherit a haunted ghost town filled with spirits who hated her family?

Lily preferred the ghost residents. Sure, an army of dead miners had shown up on the lawn to scare her into running away, but...

Never mind. She didn't prefer either town. They all hated her.

The people of Lucky Valley blamed the Goodes for every piece of bad luck that befell the locals. Like Lily just waited around, willing souf-flés to cave in and people to slip on cracked side-walks for the heck of it.

"It's not like I'm busy trying to open a busi-ness or anything," she muttered to herself, "inviting strangers into my home so I can support my family. This isn't just some bleak, bleak, terrible hobby."

For that reason, she didn't host a grand-opening party. None of the townsfolk would have attended.

Hello, sir?

Lily wasn't sure where the whisper was coming from, only that the male voice had invaded her mind off and on for the last week. No matter how she tried to find the source, in the end it was just a whisper of a thought. At first, she believed it was a gnome. Then she assumed it was the feral cat hanging around. Now she was concerned it was a sign of madness.

"Go away," Lily whispered to the chubby-faced gnome still staring at her. She stood in the living room before a small check-in desk she'd set up near the wall. From her location, she could see across an antique couch past the front hall into the library. The vantage point showed anyone coming in or out of the front door.

Nothing in the home felt like it belonged to her. Sometimes she wished the antique furniture would break and stay broken, especially the couch. That ugly thing's legs had come out from under it and yet there it was, standing as good as the day it was made…back in the 1800s.

Lily sighed as she studied the guest registry.

Until the cabins were repaired (or she started kicking people out), her houseful of family left her with three rooms to rent out of a seven-bedroom, three-story home.

"Hey, Lily, want some coffee?"

Lily glanced up as Mara passed through the living room. Her sister wore pajama pants and a crop top as she stumbled toward the kitchen in fuzzy slippers. Going after her, Lily grabbed her arm, "Dammit, Mara, I told you we had guests staying here. You can't walk around like that anymore."

"Uh, yeah I can. You said to pretend I *am* a guest here and to talk up the place," Mara countered. She gestured to her outfit. "If I'm paying for a room, I'll wear what I want."

"You're not paying for anything, pickle," Lily reminded her. "Just put a bra on, for heaven's sake. The Elliotts have a kid with them."

"He's eighteen." Mara dismissed the concern. "Trust me. He'll leave you a good internet rating after meeting me."

I can see why our mother locked you up for most of...

Dammit. No. No, that was mean. She couldn't think things like that.

"Just wear a bra, please," Lily whispered.

"I will if you and Polly stop calling me pickle," Mara countered.

Lily doubted that would ever happen. "And leave the scones for the real guests. I swear the baker charges extra because I'm a Crawford-Goode."

"Yeah, probably." Mara shrugged. "Why do you think I use a fake name?"

"There is cereal in the pantry," Lily insisted.

"No, Herman ate it all last night," Mara said.

"Lobsters don't eat cereal," Lily answered.

"Then it was the raccoon," Mara called, "or that cat of yours."

The feral nuisance that kept staring at Lily was supposed to be her familiar, at least according to Polly. The cat didn't act very friendly, and on some level it made sense that Lily's familiar would be grumpy and unsociable.

Lily went back to the registry and stared at it as if her intense focus would change her circumstances—three rooms to rent out and a family to support.

Vanessa Jensen had left early, and in a huff, because she thought someone had been rummaging around in her room. Evidently, they'd re-arranged her towels and done a long list of other things that couldn't be proven. Her anger had seemed disproportionate to the situation.

"Thanks for the one star, Vanessa," Lily

muttered. That little sad rating stared at Lily every time she looked up her bed-and-breakfast online. The review had been just as scathing, *"Tacky décor, character actors on staff, and boring locale only outdone by the indifference of management to the invasion of privacy issues I encountered. A definite must-avoid."*

Lily etched an x by the woman's name and then sighed deeply, momentarily pitying herself.

Vanessa had been replaced by the truck driver Earl "Willy" Williams, who snored so loud the Elliotts complained. Willy reported that he'd lost a silver flask which he was certain had been on his nightstand but now it wasn't. Otherwise, he appeared fairly happy…and not the kind to leave online reviews.

The Elliotts were polite, in a bland sort of way. The wife smiled, the husband said things about birds or something, but after each conversation, Lily could barely remember what they'd talked about. Their son clearly had a crush on his phone. Lily had caught Frank Jr. taking selfies with several of the gnomes…some in highly questionable positions. The Elliotts were her best shot at a five-star to counteract Vanessa's angry review. Mrs. Elliott was missing a single diamond earring, but so far thought maybe she'd lost it and wasn't blaming the B&B.

Lily glanced toward the door. Chubby Face had disappeared.

Finally, there was Janice Foster, who basically kept to herself as she typed on her laptop, moving from room to room as if she couldn't quite settle on a location to work. She hardly spoke except to ask politely for fresh towels, and that the staff be on the lookout for her favorite pen—a platinum-coated fountain pen that had been a gift from someone she'd rather not name for fear of looking pretentious, but he was a famous horror author.

This was Lily's life now.

"Miss Goode?" Marion Elliott spoke softly as she gave a worried smile.

Lily glanced up at the woman and reminded herself to return the smile. "Yes?"

"I'm sorry to bother you, but have you seen my son?"

"Oh, ah…" Lily glanced around as if that limited view would give her answers. "No, I don't think he's been down for breakfast yet."

"That's so strange." She gave a small frown, sighing. "Okay, thank you."

Lily observed the woman as she looked help-lessly around the living room. "Is something the matter?"

"He didn't come in last night," Marion said.

11

"His bed doesn't look like it was slept in. It's not like him to make his bed."

Lily thought of Mara and did her best to keep smiling. "Maybe he fell asleep somewhere. The weather was beautiful last night. Let me ask around for you."

Junior hardly seemed like the camping type, unless camping was code for kegger with class-mates. The suggestion seemed to calm Mrs. Elliott some and Lily went to look for Mara. She found her sister leaning against the kitchen counter eating a scone.

At Lily's appearance, Mara pushed the pastry fully into her mouth, puffing out her cheeks. She gave an innocent grin even as she struggled to chew.

"Dammit, Mara," Lily whispered.

"What?" The word was muffled by food. She struggled to swallow before managing to add, "I was hungry. Just have Polly pull more out of her magic picnic basket."

That wasn't the point.

"Seriously, Lil. Stop being a freak," Mara scoffed. "Polly said that we could magically lift a barn and do all these fixes in like an afternoon if we pooled our powers. Who needs the stupid bakery if they're going to overcharge you? We can make our own out of thin air and—"

"We're doing this my way," Lily interrupted. "Limited magic until we fully understand the consequences involved. Where do you think that food comes from that Polly magically pulls out of her basket? For all we know, we're taking it out of a hungry kid's mouth."

"You're kind of a downer. You know that, right?" Mara said. "You need to chill."

Remembering why she'd gone to the kitchen in the first place, Lily asked, "Is Frank Jr. in your room?"

Mara looked stunned for a few seconds before snorting with laughter. "Is that a joke?"

"Junior didn't go to his room last night, and you come down all…" Lily gestured at Mara's lack of clothes.

"So clearly I slept with an eighteen-year-old," Mara answered, losing a bit of her cocky attitude.

"Well, if the bra fits…"

"Wow." Mara shook her head. "I didn't figure you for such a prude. I'll go put on a damned bra, but let's get something straight. I may be messed up, but I didn't seduce Junior. Maybe he didn't go back to his room because he's eighteen and sleeping in the same room with your parents at that age is weird."

Lily kept herself from answering, *How would*

13

any of us know if that was weird or not? You were born in a barn and I was abandoned outside an Iowa fire station with Dante and Jesse.

Marigold had done a number on all of them.

"I'm sorry," Lily said. "I'm trying. I truly am."

"I don't need your pity," Mara quipped. "I'll be sure to tell my new lover you're looking for him if I see him."

Mara stormed from the kitchen and Lily heard angry footsteps as her sister ran upstairs. The woman acted like an adolescent.

Maybe Nolan had seen the teenager.

"I can do this," Lily whispered, not believing her own mantra. She leaned against the kitchen counter and closed her eyes, trying not to let her stress get the better of her. She felt the energy coming from the walls, it pulsed, as if an extension of herself. It fed her magic. "I can do this. I can be a business owner. I can take care of my family. I can do this. I can—"

"Oh, hey, baby, how long have you been there? I didn't see you come out," Nolan said. "What can you do?"

I can do this.

Lily felt the cool breeze on her skin before she opened her eyes.

Dammit. Dammit. Dammit.

Her magic had transported her out to the cottage. Nolan stood in the doorway. He held a nail gun attached to a long orange extension cord that ran several feet across the yard from the back of the house to the cottage where he was doing repairs.

"I *hope* no one saw me come out here," Lily muttered.

Instantly understanding, Nolan set the nail gun down and moved toward her. "What's wrong? You only teleport when you're highly emotional."

"It doesn't matter," Lily dismissed, not really keen on being called highly emotional. "Have you seen the Elliott kid around anywhere this morning? His mother is searching for him."

Nolan shook his head. "No, but I haven't been looking for him either."

"He's probably with the missing flask, and pen, and whatever else has been stolen."

Sweat beaded his brow and sawdust clung to his neck. The man had an animal magnetism, no doubt about it. "Someone still taking shiny objects? Frank Jr. is hardly shiny."

"His phone is."

"Or do you mean you have reason to believe he's our thief?" Nolan asked.

"If I were a teenager, I'd probably steal a liquor flask," Lily said.

"Can't say I would've passed that up myself," Nolan agreed. "Now we just have to prove it and make him give it back."

"Any idea where he is?" Lily asked.

"The last time I saw the kid, he was marking the frame of the new barn."

"Marking? You mean he was pee—*oh, gross*," Lily said. "What in the hell was I thinking, inviting people into my home?"

Nolan's smile faded some. She supposed she should have said *our* home. It's like her mouth was trying to help her brain self-sabotage her relationship any way it could.

"Do you need me to hunt him down?" he offered.

"Yes. Yes, I would like you to hunt him down like a wolf after a bunny rabbit. I'm sure his mother would love that," Lily drawled sarcastically.

Nolan let his eyes flash with the threat of a shift as he grinned. He held his arms to the side. "Never say I didn't offer to help."

Nolan looked as if he would kiss her, and she turned her head to the side, pretending something in the forest caught her attention.

"Did I do something to piss you off?" he asked.

"No. It's just...Mara." Lily knew it was wrong to deflect her confusing feelings over her relationship onto Mara, but the woman was an easy scapegoat. Nolan hadn't really liked Mara from the beginning. Though, neither had Polly, and Polly liked everyone.

"What did she do now?"

"Ate all my scones and didn't wear a bra." Lily waved her hand in dismissal.

"You know you can kick her out. No one said you had to let her freeload off you." This was becoming an old argument. "They're all adults. You shouldn't be the one carrying the workload."

Lily went to peek inside the cottage to check the progress. The small cabin had a single bedroom, bathroom, and living room. Nolan was adding a small kitchenette adjoining the living room. An identical cabin stood close by. It was being used for storage and the remodel hadn't been started yet.

"I need to get back." Lily wasn't going to try to explain the importance of family to him. Their mother had abandoned all of her children in one form or another. Lily grew up taking care of her siblings, fighting to keep them all together.

She wasn't going to give up on Mara. That is what Marigold would have done.

Lily was not her mother.

"I need you to hear me on a couple of points and then I'll drop it," Nolan said. "I know you said Dante was looking for a job, but until that happens he needs to help you out more. I'm not just talking about running errands to town to pick up some bath towels or helping you find a pen to write with when you're on the phone."

"He'll help if I ask him to," Lily said.

"But you never ask him to."

She hated that he had a point.

"I don't even think Mara is looking for a job. I don't like how she tries to guilt you for what your mother did to her," Nolan continued. "I know Polly offers all the time, but I will say, I get why you don't ask your aunt for more help."

"Can we not fight?" Lily asked. "Let's just get through this opening. This is all so new to everyone. It will settle. I'll figure out a way my siblings can help out more."

"I'm not trying to put more pressure on you," he said.

Lily nodded. That may be the case, but she felt the pressure.

"Want to go into town tonight for dinner?"

he asked. "Could be good to get out of the house."

"Can't leave." Lily followed the orange extension cord back toward the house. Quietly, she added, "And you're one to talk. You're the highly emotional one, wolf boy."

Nolan laughed. She knew his shifter hearing would pick up her words.

He called after her, "I wondered if you were going to let me get away with that comment."

CHAPTER TWO

"LUGWICK, I want you to tell me right now if you had anything to do with the disappearance of that ill-behaved young man."

Aunt Polly Crawford's voice was uncharacteristically hard, but since the woman was dressed in a pink princess gown with sparkles and wings, it was a little hard to take her anger seriously. Well, that and the fact she interrogated a garden gnome.

Lily watched the absurd scene from the doorway to Polly's third-floor bedroom. The fact the room appeared to be twice the size allowed by architectural design did cause a moment of wonder. Polly had no problem tapping into magic for everyday things. That attitude bothered Lily, who understood nothing in life came without consequences. Until she figured out what those consequences were, she wasn't going to rely on magic.

Okay, and if Lily were honest, her magic was unreliable. If she tried to stretch a room beyond its physical boundaries, she was positive it would result in a nuclear explosion.

People always dreamed of what it would be like to have superpowers and magic. Lily could say with confidence: it sucked big time.

"Answer me," Polly demanded of the gnome. "Don't make me bap you."

The statue didn't move.

Polly's hair wasn't of any natural red color, but it suited her vibrant personality. All evidence pointed to the woman being older, at the very least the same age Lily's mother would have been, but Polly's face only showed a hint of those years.

"I don't think he knows anything," Lily drawled.

"Don't let the cute face fool you. He's a sneaky one." Polly sighed. "But perhaps you're right. We both know Herman is the mastermind between the two of them."

Herman was Polly's enchanted pet lobster. More often than not, the crustacean was in the blue plastic baby pool wearing a sailor cap.

However, now small watery footprints led across the floor toward Lugwick, as if he was going to stand by his friend.

There were many times in the day that Lily looked at the surreal reality surrounding her and thought, "This is my life now."

"Herman?" Polly asked the lobster. "Where's the boy?"

"Let me know what you find out," Lily said.

Polly waved her hand without taking her eyes off her two suspects. Little pink sparkles surrounded her wiggling fingers, floating to shut the door on Lily.

"Do I even want to know?" The sarcastic drawl of Dante's voice was both familiar and comforting.

Lily shook her head in denial and rubbed the bridge of her nose.

Her brother carried himself in a way that denoted sophistication. It was an effect he'd culti-vated as a child. Being the skinny kid in foster care had made him an easy target for bullies. But, lying to say he was from an affluent family, and wasn't allowed to talk about it, had opened up a seat for him at the popular table.

Dante had always been smart, but he never used those brains to further himself. Instead, he drifted—from job to job, from hobby to hobby.

He always stopped himself before mastering a task. It was that way with playing guitar, when he was promoted to head waiter, when he made the varsity team in high school basketball. And because they thought he was a spoiled rich boy, everyone let him get away with it.

Giving a man like Dante powers was the ultimate enabling. He'd have an excuse not to push himself. She had a vision of her brother lying on the couch, summoning a remote to his side.

"Why are you looking at me like that?" Dante frowned.

"Thank you for being normal," Lily whispered, giving a meaningful glance at Polly's door. She reached to hug him and he ducked away with a laugh.

"Any scones left?" Dante asked, moving to go down the stairs.

"Probably not, but if any *are* left, they're for guests. Cereal is in the pantry."

"Herman ate all the cereal," Dante said. He took the stairs two at a time, rushing down before Lily could say anything more.

Lily started to follow her brother. Polly burst through the door, startling her. Purple glitter drifted in the air around her like dust. "Did I hear Florus?"

"My name's Dante," he yelled from below.

24

Polly preferred to use Dante's first name. It wasn't until the reading of the will that they'd learned Dante actually had a different first name.

"I need to question your raccoon next, Florus," Polly said. "We'll get to the bottom of this new mystery."

"Did you discover anything?" Lily asked her aunt.

"Well, they're hiding something but it's not the boy. He's in the backseat of their family car."

"Thanks." Lily knew better than to ask how Polly figured out the boy's location. She had never seen the lobster talk. She also wasn't about to ask what new mystery Polly was investigating. If it kept her aunt busy and out of trouble, Lily wasn't going to get in the way of it.

Hello, sir?

The voice was louder than before and had a decidedly masculine, out-of-breath quality.

Lily frowned, paused on the step and looked at Polly. "Did you hear that?"

"That *ping, ping, boink, ping*?" Polly asked. "Isn't it pretty?"

"No, the…" Lily would not get sucked into the madness. Not this morning. "Never mind."

"Never do." Polly winked.

Lily rushed down the steps and out the front door. The last thing she needed was a missing teenager the week of her grand opening. Well, a missing kid was always a bad thing. No one *needed* a missing teenager.

She jogged toward the Elliotts' old station wagon and cupped her eyes as she leaned into the glass. Sure enough, Frank Jr. was sprawled out on the seat. He had a black eye and a small cut on his forehead.

Lily rapped her knuckles on the window. The kid's arm twitched. She knocked louder. Tired brown eyes met hers, one of them a little bruised and bloodshot.

"It's my car," Junior mumbled. "Go away, lady. Don't you have some gnomes to polish or something?"

Lily could easily see the effects of what could have been a hangover. She knocked louder and shouted through the glass (probably a little more aggressively than necessary), "Your mother is worried about you."

The little shit flipped her off.

Excuse me, sir? Hello, sir?

Lily covered her ears and looked around. A green gnome hat poked out from the flowers along the front of the porch. Another hid, unsuccessfully, behind the wooden rails. "Omigod, stop!"

She glanced at the car window to see Frank

Jr. glaring at her.

Lily forced a smile. At least the kid was safe. Mystery solved.

She went back to the house and found Marion in the library staring out of a window. Her hands were shaking.

"He's safe," Lily assured her, not wanting her to worry.

Turning around, Marion appeared confused by the interruption. "Who's safe?"

"Your son. You told me he was missing." Lily tilted her head and watched the woman closely. Her eyes appeared a little glazed. Painkillers, maybe? "I found him sleeping in the backseat of your car. I knocked on the window, we talked," Lily paused, adding silently, *he flipped me the bird*, "and he just seems tired. He did have a cut on his head though if you want to check on him."

"Oh, that, it wasn't from a fight," Marion said, a little too quickly.

"Uh, okay." Lily nodded.

"He was running in the woods and smacked into a branch," Marion explained.

"We don't recommend running in the woods. They can be a dangerous place if you don't know where you're going," Lily said.

"He won't do it again," Marion assured her.

Great. More stuff to add to my list of things to do:

1. Post signs warning guests about getting lost in the woods so they don't sue me for their stupidity.

2. Tell parents that even though it's legal for minors to drink on private property with their parents in Colorado—or something like that—she wasn't going to allow it on her private property.

3. Keep gnomes from creeping up on the guests. Somehow stop Mara from being Mara. Make sure Dante doesn't turn into a magic-using couch potato. And stop Polly from covering everything in glitter.

Lily swiped at her arm in annoyance, willing the purple glitter away. The sparkles soaked into her skin and she began to tingle. Those weren't pieces of glitter. Her fingers began to itch and she wanted to shoot power into the sky like little fireworks.

I should probably have not entered the service industry.

"Thank you for finding him," Marion said when Lily didn't readily speak. "He's such an extraordinary boy."

For a worried mother, Marion didn't seem too eager to check on her child. Then again, if she were on opioids, that would make her current state explainable.

"Is everything all right?" Lily asked. A feeling of concern tried to bubble to the surface but was overridden by the magic forcing its way through her body. She shook her hand, trying to get the sensation to stop. It only caused the itch to become worse.

"Yes, your place is lovely." Marion nodded her head and returned to her worried post staring out of the window.

Lily balled her hand into a fist and hid it behind her back. The sensation tried to work its way up her spine.

"You know, Lucky Valley is special. If there is something you're concerned about, or need help with, we're pretty understanding around here." Even as she said it, Lily realized she sounded a little foolish but if they were dealing with a supernatural kid or something, there was a chance someone could help. She'd been told that supernatural people were drawn to Lucky Valley. And, if it was opioid addiction, Lily had seen plenty of people with that struggle in Spokane.

"You're very kind," Marion answered. "I'll suggest going into your lucky town this evening to my husband. Who knows, maybe we'll buy lottery tickets and strike it big."

Lily didn't bother to explain Lucky Valley was plagued with the opposite of good luck, and the Elliott family was currently staying at the supposed epicenter of misfortune.

Marion gazed out of the window. The itching

became painful. Lily couldn't take it any longer and flung her hand with a soft gasp.

Purple light shot from her fingertips and hit the bookshelf. Books fell onto the floor as pounding footsteps ran up the stairs.

Marion inhaled sharply at the noise but had missed the light show coming from Lily's hand. If anything, she would have seen a flash reflected in the window.

Lily made it to the bottom of the stairs in time to see Frank Jr. reaching the top. Thank goodness she hadn't summoned a noisy ghost with her misfire.

This business venture was not turning out how she'd imagined. Lily went to the bookshelf and began picking up the mess. Marion gave her a small smile before resuming her examination of the backyard. Thankfully, she looked none the wiser about the magical mishap and didn't appear concerned about the fallen books.

Moments later, Polly rushed down the stairs, pointing her finger toward the door. She no longer wore the princess dress, but a bright green A-line skirt and flouncy top. Her orange plastic glasses were shaped into cat eyes. They matched her large bracelets and clunky necklace. "Follow me."

Lily glanced up the stairs, half expecting gnomes to appear. They didn't.

Polly came back inside, grabbed Lily's arm and pulled her from the house. "I said follow me, sugar bee."

"What's going on?" Lily asked. "I found the kid. He's a jerk, but he's fine."

"You're not to worry about anything. We'll figure this all out," Polly insisted. She began leading the way around the side of the house. "Now is not the time for fear. We must remain strong."

"Oh, no, Polly, stop. Everything is fine with Nolan and me. If you're picking up anything, I'm just frustrated about—"

"I know. You and Nolan are going to be married. Dante and I have it all planned." Polly continued on her mission toward the back yard. "This is less serious, but we need to handle it. Don't worry. I already cast a spell to draw more guests, so our businesses are going to be fine."

"Our," Lily repeated, trying to hide her doubt, "businesses?"

"Oh, dear, you're in shock. Okay, I'll talk slower so you can understand. You own Garden Gnome Bed-and-Breakfast. I own Polly's Perfectly Pretty Princess Dream Getaway Extravaganza. I have a feeling it will be very popular with trolls."

"Please tell me you're kidding." Lily stopped walking halfway to the cabins. She heard the *whoomp-whoomp* of Nolan's tools.

"Why would I joke about trolls?" Polly waved her hand forward like a general leading soldiers into battle. Lily felt her feet trip forward as they tried to walk without her.

"I'm trying to cater to humans. You can't bring trolls here," Lily said, struggling against Polly's magical pull on her feet. However, it was only once she settled into a stride that she was able to regain control.

"You're cranky," Polly dismissed. "I'm going to pretend a Crawford descendent didn't say that. We do not discriminate in this family."

Polly made a beeline toward the second cabin that was being used for supply storage until the remodeling started on it.

Coldness crept over Lily as she approached, filling her with the same kind of dread she felt when watching an actress walk right into the killer's trap. Her heart began to beat a little harder. Each breath felt as if it didn't deliver enough oxygen to her lungs.

"Polly," Lily whispered, lightheaded. "I don't want to go in there."

"We can't bring in there out here," Polly insisted.

"Something's," Lily swayed, "off. Please don't make me go in."

Polly went to the door and opened it. Again Lily felt her feet moving even though she didn't command them to do so. Polly forced her into the cottage without even touching her.

"Yes, sugar bee," Polly said, her voice low. "Someone turned the poor thing off."

As Polly stepped aside, she lifted her hand to send tiny lights into the air. The soft illumination revealed dust drifting all around them. Lily followed Polly's gaze. A pale blue hand rested over a pile of two-by-fours.

Dread filled Lily. The air was hard to breathe, each intake like grains of sand entering her lungs. She wanted to run and gasp in the fresh air. She wanted to escape the presence of that hand. The fine manicure and the delicate fingers gave away that it was from a younger woman.

Jesse...

Images from the past, ones she'd buried deep, surged forward. Lily tried to push them back, but the sight of the hand caused her magic to draw childhood memories from the locked trunk in her mind. They flooded through her like boiling water, scalding a painful path from her brain to her chest.

Her vision dimmed for a brief moment before returning. The cottage was gone, replaced by a memory she rather not face. She was inside the car they had lived in as children.

As if she were no more influential to the situation than the window crank handle on the car door, she saw the past surrounding her. She heard the sound of Dante's panicked breaths. They'd both fallen asleep and Jesse was gone. Marigold had left them on some dingy corner, no more or less terrifying than any of the curbsides they'd been parked on.

Her heart squeezed. Jesse was so small. She shouldn't be on the streets by herself, not at night, not here. Lily remembered jumping out of the car, searching the sidewalks. Junkies were passed out on a stoop. A drunk sang a vaguely familiar tune, but the words were so loud and slurred they were impossible to decipher.

"Where would she go?" Dante had asked.

Lily searched in each direction. What if she were taken? What if a junkie grabbed her? What if some good Samaritan called the police and they found out Marigold hadn't been back for nearly a day?

Seeing a neon butterfly hanging over a tattoo

parlor, she pointed. Jesse loved butterflies. What two-year-old girl didn't? They both began to run.

The memory faded as she pushed the thoughts back.

Lily watched the hand, waiting for the woman to move.

"Hello?" Lily called out softly. "Are you all right?"

Please let her be all right. Please let her be—

"Oh, sugar bee, her spirit is way too new to show itself, let alone answer you right now," Polly said. "With any luck, she's not lingering around here."

Luck? Was that a joke? There was no good luck in Lucky Valley. This proved it.

Lily felt the burn of tears in her eyes. She reached forward to touch the hand. The fingers were cool. Leaning forward had brought more of the woman into view.

One-star Vanessa.

Relief that it was not Jesse filled her, which instantly made her feel guilty.

Lily searched the body for a sign of how Vanessa had died. Thoughts and fears ran rampant in her mind. Nolan had gone for a run the night before. What if the wolf took over? She'd seen firsthand how scary that could be.

No. Nolan could control his shifting if it

wasn't the full moon, and Vanessa would have been mangled if that were the case.

Lifeless eyes stared up at the ceiling from a blue-tinted face. Her limbs looked as if they'd been dropped, not placed. Lily averted her gaze.

"I know this woman," Polly said.

"Vanessa Jensen," Lily answered. "She gave us the one star because she was convinced someone had been messing with her room and she hated that there were gnomes everywhere. I assumed she called a car service to pick her up like she'd threatened because she was gone."

Too many gnomes at the Garden Gnome Bed-and-Breakfast. Who would have thought? Well, on that point, Lily agreed.

Tiny footprints were imprinted on the dusty floor near the wood. They led to and from the body. Lily leaned down to study them but their exact shapes were smeared. Though she'd never seen the gnomes move, she knew they had. Was it possible Vanessa had pissed them off and the little guys took their revenge?

Polly lifted her hand and mumbled a few words. Magic floated from the artificial lighting down over Vanessa, coating her with a glow. When it landed on the floor, it erased the tiny footprints. "Rest easy, child."

"Wait, no, Polly, look." Lily pointed at the

floor. It was too late. The evidence was gone. "What did you do?"

"A blessing," Polly said.

"There were footprints on the floor. They're gone now," Lily said.

"Are they?" Polly looked down. Lily didn't buy the innocent act.

"Did the gnomes do this?" Lily asked.

"Did the statues harm Vanessa?" Polly waved her hand as if it were a silly notion.

"What did you do?" Lily insisted. If Polly was covering up for the gnomes, she needed to know.

"I told you I gave her a blessing. I can't force her to move on, but I can give her a nudge in that direction. We don't want her haunting this place with that spotty aura she carried around, especially if she didn't like the gnomes. That wouldn't be good for anyone—ghost, gnome, human, or Herman."

Out of habit, Lily muttered sarcastically, "I'd hate for your lobster familiar to be uncomfortable."

"Exactly," Polly agreed.

"I don't want Vanessa to move on at all. Can't you do something, Polly?" Panic began to fill Lily. This town hated her. The last thing she needed was to be known for finding dead bodies the first week of her business being open. She doubted any amount of magic would undo this scandal. "We'll never recover from this. The town still hasn't forgiven us for the mining accident, and that happened in the 1800s. They'll never accept us if people die here during our first week open. If this B&B closes, not one of them will give me a job. Dante has applied everywhere that we can think of. We'll have to move back to Spokane with Jesse. This house will fall into the legal system and..." She gave a helpless wave of her hands. "She's so young. We—"

"No, sugar bee, you don't want to reanimate the dead," Polly answered, understanding what Lily was asking.

"But we're powerful. You say we're powerful all the time and this place is filled with magic," Lily insisted. "Can't we just animate her long enough to walk her somewhere else? Like Denver? They have a police force. Let them figure this out. We did nothing wrong."

"We do not want to start a deadie apocalypse," Polly stated. "It takes life to create more life, and even if we had the necessary sacrifices in mind, that life would only be temporary. She'd crave more, gaining her years by devouring the flesh of—"

"Okay, Polly, I get it." Lily held up her hands to stop the imagery. "No zombies. Then what are we going to do? It doesn't feel right hiding the body but an investigation will be the end of this place. No one will come to a murder house on vacation."

"Trolls will come." Polly tried to sound comforting and failed.

Lily knew what the right thing to do was. There was no question. She'd report it. Vanessa might have been mean-spirited and spoiled and elitist and rude, but she was still a person. None of those things said she deserved to die. Lily wouldn't pretend that she liked the woman, but someone would be looking for her. Someone would care about her. "There has to be something we can do."

"What's done is done," Polly said. "I can't control the fate of others, nor would I want to. Changing such things always has consequences that cannot be foreseen. There are forces more powerful than you or I. Death in one so young is always sad, but she will move on to where she needs to be."

"I'll call Deputy Herczeg. She owes us for saving her life after Echidna bit her." Lily felt the world crushing down on her. From the very first moment she'd heard Marigold had left her house in the middle of Colorado, a weight had dropped onto her shoulders, and every day more was added onto the pile. She had been forced to face her neglected past, to try to make peace with the mother who'd abandoned them. She was forced to learn some hard truths, and to accept a whole slew of craziness.

Lucky Valley was an opportunity to give her siblings a home, to provide them with security, a place no one could take away from them. But it seemed at every turn fate was conspiring to kick them out.

"What about the mining ghosts? Do you think they did this to drive us out of the house?" Lily asked. "They did possess Mara so she would lead them to attack us."

"No. Dante and I put a binding spell on Unlucky Valley to keep them in the mining town."

Lily took a deep breath and tried to concentrate on what she needed to do. "I'll call Herczeg and beg her to keep this quiet. I hate to ask but will you do your thing and make lunch for everyone? And don't tell them what's happening. I don't want a panic."

"You can't hide this. It's not like we're going to rewind time and undo it," Polly said.

"Can we do that?" Lily barely dared to hope.

"Yes," Polly nodded as if that were common knowledge in the witch world.

"Omigod, why didn't you say that to begin with? Let's do that. Let's rewind time."

"No." Polly shook her head in denial. "You can't neglect your powers and the lessons I try to teach you and then hope to use them when it's convenient. Your magic zips when it should zap, bips when it should bap, and gives people warts."

"I didn't give anyone warts," Lily insisted, frustrated. "Fine. You win. I'll take all the magic lessons you want me to."

"Promise?"

"Sure," Lily said, eager to get the gruesome task over with.

"Wonderful!"

"Now, let's rewind this and get Vanessa out of here."

"No.

"But—"

"The last time witches rewound time, humans ended up with noses in the middle of our faces," Polly said. "And a curse that was stopped the first time around was missed during the reset."

"I don't think that's a real story." Lily looked at Vanessa's hand.

"Of course it's a real story. I really said it." Polly patted Lily's arm. "Life has threads, and this one has snapped. You should follow yours

41

back into the house. We need to discover who did this ourselves. We can't have outsiders poking around our secrets. The house won't like that very much. It will protect itself."

"How? We're not detectives." Lily had about all the crazy she could handle for one lifetime. If all the signs pointed to run, shouldn't she listen and just pack up and run?

"We're better than detectives. We're witches." Polly led the way from the cottage and shut the door without touching it when Lily came out. "First, we need a suspect list—not me, of course, but let's see. Who would want this girl dead? There's you, for the bad review. Not Nolan. He's too gentle."

"Hey now, wait a minute. He's a werewolf who can't control his outbursts once a month and you think he's more innocent than I am?"

"You *are* pretty upset about that one star." Polly waved her hand in greeting as Nolan came out of the other cottage with his nail gun.

Nolan smiled at them and waved back.

"Why did you say this situation was less important than Nolan and my relationship?" Lily asked.

"Your children will end the Dawson curse, and there's that whole other thing." Polly waved her hand in dismissal.

"What other thing?" Lily didn't need any more pressure on her relationship. The idea of destiny made her want to run away from her life. She wanted Nolan to be with her because of her, not because of destiny and magic. Lily prided herself on her independence. She didn't like to think she was being pushed in any one direction, even when signs appeared to indicate otherwise.

Nolan's smile faltered as he stared at them.

"You know, that other thing." Polly reached into her dress pocket and pulled out Lily's phone as if she'd been carrying it all along. "Here. Call the deputy. Don't worry. I'll make sure she keeps this under wraps for now." She waved Nolan to them. "We'll see if the wolf can sniff out any clues for us."

Nolan set down the nail gun and jogged toward them. "What's going on? I can see something is off by your expressions. Is it the Elliott kid?"

"He was sleeping one off in his parents' car," Lily said. She gestured to the cottage. "This is worse."

Nolan turned to look at it, and his eyes instantly flashed with gold and he tilted his head back to take a deep breath. "Who is it?"

"The woman Lily didn't like for leaving the one star," Polly said.

"Can you stop staying that?" Lily snapped.

"The truth?"

"Yeah, stop staying *that* truth." Lily felt the urge to scream. She couldn't take much more. "Just stop. If you tell that to Deputy Herczeg I'll probably be thrown into jail...actually, yeah, tell her that. Tell her it was me. Send me to prison. It sounds awesome compared to this. I did it. Tell her it was me."

"Hey, Pol, would you give us a moment?" Nolan asked.

"I have dinner guests," Polly said, striding toward the house. "Cheeseburger pickle pie for everyone."

At this point, Lily didn't care what Polly fed them.

"Don't do anything yet," Nolan told her. "Let me look first and we'll figure this out together."

He went toward the cottage. Lily didn't wait as she lifted the phone to dial the police. She just wanted this to be over.

CHAPTER THREE

No relationship was perfect, but Nolan liked to think he was a reasonably dependable guy. He never cheated. He didn't stay out all night drinking. He enjoyed the simple things in life. He liked living with Lily, even though she was moody and had more family issues than a den of drunken goblins.

"I need you to come out here. Now. It's important."

Nolan listened as Lily placed the call to Herczeg to report the death. He didn't make it a habit to eavesdrop on conversations, but this was a big exception in the form of a poor girl lying partly on the floor, and partly on his pile of lumber.

"No, I don't want to say on the phone."

He couldn't detect any trace smell of poisons

or drugs. However, when his eyes focused in on her neck, he saw what looked to be discoloration on her skin. One of the woman's fingernails had also been torn.

"Fine, I need to report a possible accident. Or crime. Or something."

The fact she'd either fallen on the lumber or had been tossed there said whoever had done it wasn't trying to hide their crime. He'd met Vanessa when she'd checked in. Lily clearly had not liked her, if the late-night rants were any indication, but Nolan thought Vanessa had to be decent enough. Yeah, a little prissy. She tried too hard to be artificially pretty like socialites her age tended to do—too much makeup, too much perfume, an avoidance of getting their manicured hands dirty. Nolan much preferred women like Lily—well, women like Lily when she wasn't looking at him like life annoyed her.

"No I can't use my witchy powers to take care of it myself. Just get out here and do your damned job, Herczeg."

Nolan tried to be patient. She was undoubtedly dealing with a lot—new powers, the existence of the supernatural, a new business, the age-old hatred of those in town who blamed her family for every bad thing that had ever happened to them. Mara was a freeloader. Polly was loveable, but a flake. Dante was a sarcastic ass. Jesse, who he hadn't met, seemed to be pouting like a petulant child and refused to come to see the house. He'd heard Lily begging her sister to move when she thought he wasn't listening.

Fine, maybe he eavesdropped more than he should, but it's not like his girlfriend was telling him anything. Finding out personal information from her was like trying to read a grimoire written in a dead language with the pages glued shut.

There were days he wondered why he'd agreed to move into this madhouse.

And then he would see her smile at him. That was all it took. One smile and he was reminded of all that was good between them. She had a kind heart. He'd found one of her notebooks that had ideas scribbled in it. One of the pages listed what she would do if she became a millionaire and almost everything on it was taking care of other people and donating to charities.

"Seriously, you're going to make me spell it out?" Lily's voice lowered to a whisper and he had to strain to hear it. *"Fine. There's a dead body in one of my cottages. Do you want me to witch it away into a*

ravine or something? Because I don't have any other way of dealing with it."

There was a long pause.

"*Thank you*," came the exasperated end to the phone call.

Nolan walked out of the cottage. The sickening feeling of death lingered with him. He couldn't detect any ghosts, but that didn't mean anything.

"Herczeg is on her way," Lily said. For a moment, he saw vulnerability in her expression and he thought she might cry. "She was pleasant as always."

"We'll figure this out," he promised her. "You're not alone."

Lily touched his arm and squeezed lightly. "Thank you for saying so."

Polly appeared from the house to rejoin them. "The suspects will be distracted by the buffet I laid out for them. Magically distracted if you know what I mean."

"Don't call our guests the suspects," Lily muttered.

"Aren't they?" Polly returned. "They were all here when the crime was committed. My gut says the killer is close."

"I know it wasn't me, and it wasn't Dante,"

Lily said. Nolan waited for her to mention his name. She didn't.

"I can vouch for me, and..." Polly tilted her head in thought. Nolan waited for *her* to say his name when her eyes went to him. "And Herman."

A lobster? Polly vouched for a lobster.

Nolan frowned. "I didn't do it."

"Well," Polly said, "you might not have, but your wolf—"

"Is under my control until the full moon. That's not for another week." Nolan couldn't believe his own girlfriend wasn't defending him. He looked at her expectantly.

"Polly, stop that. You know it's not Nolan," Lily said. "We already said it wasn't Nolan. He was the first one off our list."

He sighed. It would have been nice if they'd let him know he was off the suspect list.

"It's not Mara," Lily added. "At least I don't think it would be Mara. She hasn't shown signs of being possessed again, has she?"

Nolan heard the sound of tires on the gravel road heading toward them. "Deputy's here."

"That was fast," Lily said.

He led the way around the house, expecting Tegan Herczeg's beat-up brown and white truck. Policing Lucky Valley wasn't an easy job and the vehicle had been attacked more than once, as evidenced by the bullet holes in the sheriff department's seal and claw marks along the truck bed. But instead of the deputy, a jeep sped down the road, kicking up gravel as the driver swerved.

"Did Stan steal a jeep this time?" Nolan grumbled. The ghost had taken his truck for a joy ride and had wedged it halfway down a ravine.

They waited as the jeep sped past the drive, skidded to a stop, and then backed up so that it could turn toward them.

The brunette driver parked at an odd angle next to the Elliotts' sedan. Large sunglasses engulfed her face. She swung her legs out of the door before hopping down onto her high heels. She wobbled a little before righting herself. The tight skirt and see-through top wasn't anything the locals would be caught wearing.

"Where can I find the manager?" she asked. She faced them but her eyes were shaded from the sunglasses. If he let the shift enter his eyes, he would have been able to see through them, but then he'd give his supernatural heritage away.

"That would be me," Lily said, "but—"

"My bags are in the back," the woman said with a tiny wave of her fingers. "Lock up when you're done."

"I'm sorry, but we don't have any vacancies," Lily insisted.

"No, it's okay. I'll share a room with my friend, Vanessa. She's already checked in." The woman took a few sashaying steps toward the house and then stopped as if noticing it for the first time. She took off her glasses and tilted back her head. Laughing, she said to herself, "Dammit, Nessa, you win this round. Freaking garden gnomes? How in the hell did you find this dump?"

"Hey," Lily said defensively.

The woman turned and looked as if she dared Lily to challenge her. After a long stare, she glanced at Nolan and smiled. He knew the look wasn't for him, but the woman was obviously used to men falling all over themselves to please her.

"Food's in the dining room," Polly said.

"Oh, thank goodness, I'm famished." The woman dropped her sunglasses back over her eyes and lifted her hand to hover over the railing as she moved up the steps to the front porch. "I hope you have salad. I'm on a no-meat, no-carb diet."

When the woman walked inside the house, Polly lifted her finger and wiggled it in a tiny circle. "Oops, looks like the salad is all gone.

Guess she'll have to make do with an extra-greasy burger."

Lily gave a ghost of a smile. "Sometimes, you really outdo yourself, Aunt Polly."

The sound of another vehicle drew their attention. Lily's expression fell once more, and he could see the reality of their situation crashing in on her. This time it was Deputy Herczeg who pulled up to the house.

Tegan Herczeg had a way of intimidating just by being present. She kept her long dark hair pulled back from her face, which gave her pretty features a severe expression. He'd only seen her out of her black uniform a few times. Quite honestly, it'd been a little weird, like running into a priest without his collar.

"Have you ever thought about a yellow uniform?" Polly asked Herczeg. "Something cheerier. Something that says sunshine and happiness."

"No, because I'm not a fictional superhero or a racecar driver," Herczeg answered. She started up the stairs to the house. "Where's the body?"

"Out back," Lily said.

"Nolan, make sure no one leaves," Herczeg told him. For all intents and purposes, she was the entire sheriff's department.

Sheriff Franco Tillens was more cowboy than

lawman and, being such he didn't bother with paperwork or office hours. So the majority of the work fell on Herczeg's shoulders. No one ever mentioned changing things though, because Tillens had been sheriff since all of them could remember, and Herczeg was a new girl in town. Lucky Valley was small enough, and private enough, to only hire the two officers. Supernaturals tended to have their own ideas of justice.

"I put a spell on the house," Polly said. "The guests aren't going. I have a feeling the guilty party is close. In fact, we're expecting more guests. Isn't that right, sugar bee?"

Lily sighed, having no idea who her aunt meant but assumed it was trolls. "We don't have room for anyone else."

"Where there are people, there are rooms," Polly proclaimed as if speaking a universal truth.

Herczeg didn't wait for them to lead her around back. She strode to the backyard and glanced around. "I can't believe I forgot to ask this when you called, but we *are* talking about an actual person, right? This isn't another ghost attack? Dante didn't hug a knocker spirit again, did he? I'm a little swamped in town right now and don't have time to investigate a crime that happened in the 1700s."

"She's in the cottage on the left." Lily stood

close to him but didn't touch him. Her eyes met his and the worry in her expression was palpable.

Herczeg went straight for the cottage, all business and in a hurry.

"It's going to be all right," Nolan said. "We'll figure this out."

He wasn't sure how.

Lily studied him for what felt like a long time before slowly nodding. Sometimes, he had the distinct feeling that she expected him to leave her at any moment, and no amount of reassuring her of his commitment appeared to make a difference.

Nolan had meant it when he'd said he loved her. Yeah, they'd said it early in their relationship, but so what? That's how he felt. He loved her. She moved something within him, something primal and deep. He only hoped that his love was enough to convince her that they belonged together, forever.

Herczeg came from the cottage and made her way back toward them. She pulled a notepad from her pocket. "Who is she?"

"Vanessa Jensen," Lily answered. "She was a guest. She stayed one night. I thought she checked out and left. I don't know what she's doing in the cottage or how she got here."

"She left a one-star review," Polly piped in.

54

"She didn't like it here. Lily has been upset about it."

"Mm-hm, I see." Herczeg kept writing.

"She had a difficult personality, but—" Lily tried to explain.

"How many guests do you have on the premises?" Herczeg interrupted.

As Lily listed all the guests, and told what she knew about each of them, Nolan studied the house. Frank Elliott watched them intently from the kitchen window. His eyes met Nolan's, but he didn't turn away.

"And are any of them supernatural?" Herczeg asked.

"Not that I know of," Lily said.

"No," Polly said at the same time.

"And you're sure about this?" Herczeg insisted.

"No one has said anything," Lily said.

"No, not sure," Polly answered at the same time.

The deputy glanced at the two women and sighed, before drawling, "*Rrr-ight.*" Herczeg continued her questioning. "When is the last time anyone saw Vanessa or was in that cottage?"

"We use it for storage. I've had no reason to go in there," Nolan said.

"Do you keep it locked?" the deputy asked.

"Saw no need," he answered.

"I thought she left yesterday," Lily said.

"You think? You don't pay attention to which guests are on the property?" Herczeg frowned.

"Her room was empty and she'd told me the night before she was going to leave. I assumed she left," Lily said.

"Are Mara and Dante still staying in the home?" Herczeg asked, not glancing up from her notepad.

"It wasn't us," Lily said defensively. "Why would we kill a guest? We want our business to thrive."

"You indicated she was unpleasant," Herczeg said. "Things happen."

"That's correct. Things do happen," Polly agreed.

At that, the deputy directed her gaze at Lily. "Did something happen?"

Lily stiffened. "You mean, did I infect the girl with bad luck and cause this?"

"Well…" That was exactly what Herczeg had been implying. "Unfortunate incidences have been on the rise."

"Since the Goodes came back into town, you mean." Lily ran her hand through her hair and shook her head. "This is unbelievable. I am so tired of being blamed every time someone falls out of a tree or trips on the sidewalk."

"I wouldn't compare a dead body in your cottage to a simple mishap," Herczeg said.

"Neither would I." Lily closed her eyes and took a deep breath. When she opened them, they were glassy, as if she held back tears. "The truth is, I don't know if I have a bad luck curse, and I don't know if that has anything to do with this, but I do know I didn't hurt that woman."

When Herczeg would have again written something, Lily slipped her hand over the notepad to stop her.

"Tegan, please. This will ruin us. I need this business to work for my family. I'm trying so hard to fit in around here. I don't know what else I can do." She pulled her hand from the notepad. "But I do know that you owe us. We helped you when we didn't have to."

"And I appreciate your having saved my life, but as a deputy, I can't make exceptions to—" Herczeg began.

"We're not asking you to ignore what's happened," Nolan put forth, stopping Lily before she could try to bribe the deputy. It wouldn't work. Herczeg was too honest. "We're asking you to please be as discreet as possible and don't say it was murder, or bad luck, until you have solid proof. Polly already cast a spell to keep everyone here. Conduct your investigation at the house. Don't drag anyone into town for questioning. Don't tell Caroline at the paper."

Herczeg sighed and looked around the open landscape. "Sheriff has the final say."

"We both know he's camping and won't be back for days. I'd be surprised if you can even get ahold of him." Nolan placed a hand on her shoulder. "We'll fully cooperate with you. I give you my word."

Herczeg thought about it.

"I'll owe you," Nolan said.

"I'll try to keep it quiet as long as I can." Herczeg slipped the notepad into her pocket. "I can't vouch for the coroner though. You know as well as I do these things have a way of getting out."

"Tell Dr. Cole you need her to keep it under wraps," Nolan said. "If it comes from you, she'll listen. She takes her job seriously."

"We can help," Polly said. "Let us help. You said you have your hands full with town business, and with the sheriff gone, you'll need all the assistance you can get."

"Fine," Herczeg said reluctantly.

"Deputy Polly reporting for duty," Polly said, saluting.

"I'm not deputizing you," Herczeg clarified. "No offense, but I'd deputize Herman before I gave that kind of authority to…" Her words faltered and she appeared to rethink her comment. "To someone without the sheriff's say so."

"Can I have a badge? No need to give me a gun. I have my fingers." Polly shot her fingertips like play weapons. "*Pew-pew-pew!*"

"No." Herczeg pulled out her phone. "I'm going to call Dr. Cole and get her out here to start forensics. Then I'll need to question everyone who was here."

"I thought Dr. Cole was the coroner," Lily said as Herczeg dialed her phone.

"She is. She's also the most qualified to collect any crime scene evidence," Nolan explained. "We don't get much call for crime scene techs around here. I can't even tell you when the last murder happened in Lucky Valley."

"We don't know that it's murder," Lily whispered. "Maybe she tripped."

"I saw her neck," Nolan answered, just as softly. "I'd be surprised if it was accidental."

"And this is my life," Lily mumbled to herself. "I need to find Dante and let him know what's happening. Please try to keep Herczeg reined in.

No crime scene tape or flashy signs. That Elliott kid will have it posted all over the internet in a heartbeat."

Nolan nodded that he had heard her. Lily ran toward the back door to get her brother.

"Can I arrest someone?" Polly asked, lifting her hands like a bad television ninja.

"No," Herczeg stated flatly between statements to Dr. Cole.

"But what if there's a perp? Can I take him down?" Polly asked.

"No," the deputy answered.

"I changed my mind. Can I have a weapon?" Polly kicked her foot a few feet off the ground and struck what was probably intended to be a frightening pose. It wasn't.

"No," Herczeg said, again pausing her conversation. "Absolutely not."

"Handcuffs?"

"No."

"Can I have a chicken?" Polly asked.

"What?" Herczeg snapped in irritation as she hung up the phone. She lifted her hand. "Stop asking me questions or I'll have you arrested for impeding an investigation."

"Boy oh boy." Polly sidled up next to Nolan and whispered, "That woman really doesn't like chickens."

CHAPTER FOUR

MURDER.

Dr. Olive Cole's proclamation hung over Lily's head like a noose. With that one word, there was no discreet way of taking Vanessa from the property. The victim might not have been the nicest person, but Lily still felt responsible for her. She'd been a guest in Lily's home and now she was dead.

Murder.

It was impossible to wrap her mind around that word.

"How can you know?" Lily asked. Surely it was too soon to be certain.

She had not met any other coroners, but she could well imagine they were odd people by default. It would take a specific type to go into such a field. Dr. Cole definitely fit into the odd category. Her short dark hair had a pixie cut that accentuated her small figure. Rectangular glasses framed her eyes, giving her black skinny jeans and black long-sleeve shirt an almost beatnik feel. Lily wouldn't have been shocked if she pulled out a copy of Jack Kerouac and began reading.

When Dr. Cole didn't answer, Lily repeated louder, "How can you be sure it's murder?"

The question appeared to offend the woman.

"I mean, don't you have to do an autopsy or something?" Lily insisted. "People have accidents all the time."

"Uh, Lily." Nolan lifted his hand as if to dismiss the question for her. Quietly, he explained, "Dr. Cole's father is a spriggan."

Did the man think that sentence made logical sense?

"Um, okay?" Lily gestured her hands in a cross between irritation and confusion. "What the hell is a sprig man?"

"Spriggan," Nolan corrected. "They're fairy-like creatures who guard graveyards. They know death. If she says murder, it's murder."

"It's murder. I can smell it," Dr. Cole stated, "and feel it."

"That poor dear," Polly whispered.

Lily rubbed her eyes as tears threatened. A

wave of empathy and sorrow filled her. How could she not feel bad about this? "Accidents are hard enough, but to be killed so young…" Her words tapered off as she eyed Dr. Cole. "Can you tell us who did it? Or why they did it here?"

"Those exact details would be her job." Dr. Cole motioned to Deputy Herczeg. "But I can tell you how. She was strangled. It doesn't take a spriggan or a genius to figure that one out." The woman scratched the back of her head, messing up her hair before smoothing it down once more. "So, can I ask what she did to make you mad?"

Lily frowned. "Who said she made me mad?"

Dammit, Polly. Her aunt needed to stop telling people about the one star like it was some kind of motive. If Lily were put on trial in Lucky Valley, the jury of her peers would probably find her guilty before the trial even started. She'd be burned at the stake.

"Aren't you a powerful witch?" Dr. Cole insisted. "You *are* Lily Goode, aren't you? Everyone in town is talking about the bad luck curse you put on us. This is just part of that, right? It'd be helpful if you let me know as a courtesy. I know you witches have a way of covering your tracks, and there is no reason for me doing fifteen hours' worth of work to help

63

solve a murder that can't be solved with forensics."

Great. So even if the evidence didn't point at her, it would still point at her.

"I didn't curse anyone," Lily protested. "I wish people would stop saying that. I don't want to spread bad luck. I want a lot of things, but cursing people is not on the list."

Surprisingly, it was the deputy who came to her defense when she said, "I believe her."

"Thank you," Lily said in exasperation.

Herczeg wrote on her notepad and muttered to the doctor out of the side of her mouth, "Her magic is all over the place. A real hot mess. I doubt she could cover her tracks yet."

"Seriously?" Lily questioned in exasperation. They were going to make fun of her now?

The deputy shrugged. "That's what Polly said."

Herczeg's phone buzzed and she glanced down at it, not answering.

"I didn't," Polly countered. "I said your magic was misfiring like a teenage boy on a prom date."

"That is so much worse," Lily answered.

"You promised me you'd start practicing, so we'll have you shipshape and top deck ready in no time." Polly grabbed hold of her by the face and patted several times.

Lily flinched and drew her head away just as Polly began to pinch her cheeks. She swatted the woman's hand away. "I don't even know what that means."

"Ready to perform in public. Haven't you ever been on a cruise ship?" Polly waved her hand in dismissal. "You need to get out more."

Booking a cruise and being dropped off on some remote dock sounded like a good plan. Belize, maybe? She knew very little about Belize other than it was in Central America. At least she was pretty sure that was where it was located. Perhaps she should travel farther south, to some place this craziness couldn't follow her. Antarctica?

Severe cold washed up over her legs at the thought and she felt her magic beginning to pull her. Her heart pounded much harder than it should have.

"No. Stop," she cried out, lifting her hands as if that would anchor her. If she teleported herself to the South Pole, she'd be dead instantly.

"No, I won't stop," the deputy denied. "I'll do my job."

"Not you," Lily said, feeling her magic

subsiding. Thankfully, she'd not gone anywhere. "Me."

Herczeg dropped her hands to her hips, still holding her notepad. "You do realize your odd behavior makes you highly suspect, don't you?"

"I didn't do anything wrong," Lily insisted. "Why would I harm someone and then hide the evidence in the last place I'd want a crime committed?"

"I can think of reasons," Polly said.

"Stop. Helping." Lily lifted the flat of her hand in front of Polly's face.

"Then stop asking questions." Polly gave Lily's blockade a high-five.

Lily dropped her hand. Herczeg's phone vibrated again, and again the deputy glanced at it and ignored it.

"So what happens next?" Exhaustion filled every corner of her being. Lily wanted to crawl into bed and not wake up. Was there some kind of spell to make that happen? Fairytale princesses were falling under sleeping curses all the time.

Lucky women.

Her toes began to tingle and the sensation rushed up her body. Her hair lifted slightly but there wasn't a breeze.

"What's she doing?" Herczeg asked.

"Is that smoke?" Dr. Cole questioned. "Is she setting herself on fire?"

Nolan grabbed Lily and pulled her against his chest. "Whoa, easy."

"That's not good," Polly said. "You shouldn't be drawing in the bad magic like that."

Lily shivered as the tingling subsided. It left her weaker than before.

"I need to talk to everyone who's staying on the property." Herczeg again glanced at her phone as it buzzed.

Hello, sir?

The male voice was back. Lily looked around to see if anyone else noticed it. They didn't. However, the feral black cat was on the roof of the cottage looking down at them.

"I could use help carrying the body to my van," Dr. Cole said. Lily glanced back to the group. The doctor was looking pointedly at Nolan. "You up for it?"

Nolan nodded. "Drive your vehicle around."

Dr. Cole went to get her van. Lily glanced at the roof but the cat was gone.

"How do you want to do this?" Lily asked.

"As fast as possible," Herczeg answered. "Nonemergency calls are already backing up. They're going to keep coming and those people will get angrier with each passing hour. Then they'll start calling my boss. Eventually, they're going to come out here to see what's going on. If the sheriff asks me, I can't lie about it."

As if to prove her point, her phone vibrated again.

"Anything a code enforcer can do?" Nolan asked. Until very recently, he'd been the local code enforcement officer, which was more of an official title to an unofficial job. It was in that capacity that Lily had met him. He'd been trying to nuisance code her into abandoning her inheritance at the behest of the local politicians.

"I thought you quit," Herczeg said. "All the calls have been rerouted to the sheriff's department."

"Do you care about my employment status?" Nolan arched a brow. "Or do you want my help?"

Lily found she didn't like the friendly way Nolan smiled at the deputy but clenched her teeth to keep from saying anything about it. She also didn't like the idea of him leaving while Herczeg was investigating the house.

"All right," Herczeg said, handing over her phone. "Be my guest. Hellspawn Tattoo is under siege for misspelling one of the Carter twins' names on his wife's left buttock. Questionable smells are wafting from Cold Hearth Bakery.

Fairies are having a gathering without a permit and have turned Poseidon Park into a thorn hazard."

"Can't you call a landscaper?" Lily asked. Thorns? Really?

"Poisonous thorn den," Nolan explained. "They lock themselves inside and become drunk on their own magic. It's chaos if they're left in there too long."

"Well, that stings," Polly said.

"The thorns?" Lily asked.

"They didn't invite me." Polly sighed and looked hurt by the slight.

"It's a good thing, too, or I wouldn't have your help here," Lily said.

"Quite right." Polly perked up. "It's possible the fairies are protecting themselves. This could be bigger than I first imagined."

"Bigger than murder?" Lily questioned, doubtful.

"It could be the beginning of something." Polly frowned in thought. "That poor girl could be the start. Have you seen chickens walking backward?"

"What is it with you and chickens?" Herczeg mumbled.

"Truth spell," Lily said, staring at the cottage. "Polly. Can't we make them all tell the truth?"

"You don't want that," Polly said. "It's messier than you think."

"You're wrong. I do want that," Lily said. "It can't get any messier than this. What's the point of being a witch if our magic doesn't do anything useful? If we can't help bring that woman peace or justice?"

"The safest way is by potion, and that takes time to brew, and time to grow, and time to change, and then *wham-bim-bam-boom*, you'll hear more confessions than a bartender in a beach bar kiosk." Polly plugged her ears with her index fingers. "Those are images you can't erase."

The sound of Dr. Cole's van broke through the conversation. Lily glanced at the kitchen window. Mr. Elliott stood next to his wife, staring at them. Thankfully, the vehicle didn't announce the fact the coroner owned it.

"Can we distract the guests while this is happening?" Lily nodded toward the house. "I don't want them seeing the…*her*."

"Yep," Herczeg agreed. "Let's go inside."

CHAPTER FIVE

POLICE WORK WAS the very definition of tedious.
It wasn't like on television where an editor could
cut out the hours of protests, the excuses, and
explanations about things no one even asked
about. There was no script that led the way to a
logical conclusion. It was just a mess, a maze with
no way out.

Lily had enough about fifteen minutes in, and
that was four hours ago. Why Herczeg had let
her listen in was beyond her. Maybe it was
because she wanted it so badly, her magic made
the deputy not take notice of her presence. Or
perhaps law enforcement rules were a little lax in
Lucky Valley.

They sat in the dining room. Three garden
gnomes were lined up alongside a wall. Dante

and Polly were charged with keeping everyone from wandering off or coming to eavesdrop on the conversations.

For some reason, the light coming from the fixture seemed to be a little more directly aimed at the chair of the suspect. The room temperature also heated up. It might have been Lily's imagination, but more likely it had something to do with Polly's new (perceived) role as a private investigator. Her aunt wore a dark suit with a short orange tie. Her hair was done up in finger waves like a 1920s gun moll. It only made sense that the woman had altered the environment to mimic her mood.

"Once he's out, he's out," Marion said of her husband. "He didn't get out of bed last night, or the night before."

"Marion? She was cross-stitching," Frank said with a small smile when Herczeg questioned where his wife was the night before. "It's how she spends every evening. When I get home from work, she's got supper on the table, then we watch one of our programs, and then she cross-stitches. Mostly birds. Sometimes, if it's a special night, we'll have a half glass of wine, but we naturally haven't done that while we've been here."

There was more, but Lily spaced off while he

spoke. That kept happening with the man. He was just so…droning.

Incidentally, both parents said their son was with them, even though Lily knew for a fact the alibi was a lie. Frank Jr. agreed to that lie and appeared more annoyed about being taken away from his phone than being suspected of a crime. Herczeg had confiscated all the phones. The kid was twitchy without his.

The second she'd found out there had been a murder, Janice Foster turned the interview around. The writer asked more questions than she answered as if she were suddenly writing a book on the subject. Herczeg had to stop her from jotting down notes during the interview. Lily later caught a glimpse of the woman writing furiously in a notebook and talking to the other guests. The book practically wrote itself.

Garden Gnome B&B: Bed, Breakfast, and Murder.

Truckdriver Willy appeared to be the least rattled. He kept his hands folded in his lap and gave the shortest answers possible when asked a direct question, one of the most substantial answers being, "I didn't see or hear nothin'."

"But you did arrive for your reservation a night early, didn't you?" the deputy pointed out.

"I did," Willy said.

"You have to give me more than that," the deputy insisted.

Willy seemed to consider his options, before finally explaining, "I had a load that I'm picking up get delayed and I needed a place to stop for a few nights. I found this place online. Miss Goode told me she had a room opening up and let me park my rig. She also let me come inside for dinner and relax in the library. I dozed in a chair, but ultimately, I slept in the cabin connected to my truck. I didn't see Vanessa."

Then there was Sabrina Hills, Vanessa's newly arrived friend. The socialite pretense faded quickly with the news. Sabrina evoked the most sympathy and appeared genuinely shocked by the death.

"I should have come sooner," Sabrina whispered. The sound of shaky breathing caught Lily's attention. "But it was a shot at a Hubert Gutierrez fashion show, you know. Vanessa said she understood. The second it didn't work out, I hopped in the car and came out to console her."

"Why did she need consoling?" Herczeg awkwardly handed the woman a tissue.

Sabrina sniffed again and dabbed at her eyes. "I told her not to let Brett string her along like that. Brett Wilson is her on-again-off-again pseudo-boyfriend." Sabrina cried harder. "*Was her...*"

Her voice cracked and the words were lost in a series of gasps and whimpers. The deputy handed her another tissue. Lily patted the woman's shoulder.

"She said he broke up with her for good this time. He chose the job, you know," Sabrina continued. "That's what he said, but I think it was someone else. There's always someone else. You don't dump someone as beautiful as Vanessa without there being someone even prettier, you know?"

Lily nodded when Sabrina looked expectantly at her. She assumed this could have accounted for Vanessa's one-star mood during the stay.

"You know?" Sabrina insisted.

"Oh, uh, yeah, I know." Lily nodded harder, telling the woman what she wanted to hear.

"Right?" Sabrina demanded though it might have been rhetorical.

"Yeah," Lily said. When the woman turned away from her, Lily shrugged in answer to Herczeg's slightly arched brow.

"I can't do this." Sabrina stood and rushed from the dining room.

"Do you want me to chase after her?" Lily asked.

The deputy shook her head. "I asked Polly to stall all the cars. We're good. She's not running far in those heels."

"I meant because she's upset," Lily clarified.

"And you think you're the one to comfort her?" Herczeg asked. "You don't radiate caring."

"That's a mean thing to say. I care about things," Lily defended.

"So do I, but we don't show it like other people. If you want to comfort her, send Polly." Herczeg's tone was matter-of-fact. Lily hated that the woman was right. She'd never been accused of being overly touchy-feely.

"That's everyone," Lily said. "Now what?"

Herczeg sighed in frustration and pushed her bangs back as she held her forehead. "Where were you last night?"

"You mean between cursing Lucky Valley with bad luck and trying to enact Crawford-Goode world domination?" Lily arched a brow. "I was sleeping."

"With Nolan?" Herczeg clarified.

"That's inappropriate," Lily answered.

"Do you alibi him?"

"Oh, yeah, we were…" Lily thought about Nolan leaving for a run.

"Sleeping?" the deputy prompted when Lily didn't finish her sentence.

"Mm-hmm." Lily nodded.

"Excuse me, but we're having a little car trouble. I'd like to call a mechanic." Frank Elliott appeared in the dining room doorway. "You took our phones."

"Mr. Elliott, you're not allowed to leave right now," the deputy said.

"But we've told you everything we know," Frank answered. "I hope you catch whoever did this."

"There you are, Mr. Elliott." Polly appeared next to him. "Your wife has set up a board game for you in the library."

Frank mumbled in protest, but Polly ushered him out of the dining room with a sweep of her hand. "There are snacks. Your favorite."

"We're having tuna salad finger sandwiches with ketchup and soy sauce?" Frank asked.

"Oh, um, okay," Polly nodded.

"Wait, Polly." Herczeg stopped her when she would follow Frank. "What were you doing last night?"

"Dancing naked in the moonlight. Herman can vouch for me." Polly pointed at the three gnomes. It was then Lily saw Herman hiding behind them in the shadows.

"Did you see anything?" Herczeg asked, only to amend quickly when Polly opened her mouth, "Anything useful to this case?"

Polly closed her mouth and shook her head before saying, "Well, wait. I saw crows. I thought it was four, but it could have been five or six."

Hello, sir?

Lily took a deep breath, determined to ignore the voice. "Where's Dante?"

"I sent him with Mara to bless the grounds. We'll be safe as long as we all stay in this house," Polly assured her. "And I put Sabrina in Mara's room. Mara can bunk with me."

"I can't force the guests to stay here," Lily said. She glanced at Herczeg. "Can I?"

"No. I can insist they stay, but if anyone bothers to talk to a lawyer, things will get complicated. The best we can hope for is that everyone cooperates."

"Don't worry about that. I have an itinerary all set up," Polly said. "I charmed the board games. They'll be playing for hours. A lot can be revealed by how a person crosses the enchanted forest. Then this evening, we'll have a nice scary thunderstorm with almost hurricane winds—"

"Uh," Herczeg lifted a finger as if to stop Polly.

"—followed by some downed trees and

blocked roads. Tomorrow, I'll cast a fairy enchantment. Then——"

"Polly, that sounds dangerous," Lily said.

"Which part?" Polly quirked a brow.

"All of it," Lily stated.

"Says the lady who wanted me to make deadies," Polly scoffed.

Lily stared after Polly. She felt Herczeg standing beside her. "Please wake me up and tell me I'm dreaming, or this is a bad prank. Tell me there's not a dead body in the cottage."

"There's not. They moved it." The deputy patted her shoulder. "Sorry."

A hard thud caused Lily to jump in surprise and look up. The sound of running feet pounded overhead and then down the stairs.

"My necklace!" Sabrina screeched. The sound of her voice drew a crowd from the library as she charged Lily and the deputy who was standing in the front hall. "It's gone! Someone rifled through my bags and stole my gold and sapphire necklace." She turned toward the other guests. "Which one of you did it?"

She angled her body to look at Willy, clearly choosing him as the most likely suspect by appearances alone.

"Don't look at me. I already reported I was

missing a flask." Willy gave a side-eyed glance to Frank Jr.

"I'm missing an earring," Marion said, stepping slightly in front of her son.

Janice stood with her arms crossed over her chest. She lifted her hand. "Platinum fountain pen."

"Costume jewelry, a flask, and a pen?" Sabrina scoffed. "My necklace is worth five thousand dollars. Officer," she looked expectantly at Herczeg, "I demand you check everyone's bags, and rooms, and cars, and..." Sabrina looked around the group. "Frisk them!"

"Are you sure you brought it with you?" the deputy asked.

"I don't think frisking people is necessary," Marion said.

"Why? Do you have something to hide?" Sabrina demanded.

"Hey, take it easy," Lily ordered. If Herczeg wasn't going to step in, she would. "We'll not get anywhere pointing fingers at each other."

"You're one to talk," Sabrina quipped. "I don't know what kind of unsafe, den-of-thieves horror show you're running here, but..."

The words trailed off with a sob.

More footsteps sounded upstairs, softer than Sabrina's had been. Lily glanced up and then around the group to see if anyone else heard them.

"We're leaving," Frank said. "Honey, get your things."

"But the car..." Marion began.

"I'm with you." Willy gave Lily a small nod. "I'm sorry, ma'am, but this is my cue to go."

"Do you think you can give us a ride?" Frank asked.

"Frank, no," Marion whispered.

"You can't leave," Lily said. If they left like this, there would be no salvaging this place. And, on a more serious note, one of them might be a killer. They couldn't let a killer go free.

"You have to arrest us if you want to keep us," Sabrina said. Her eyes were rimmed with red. "I know my rights."

"I believe they have seventy-two hours," Janice said. "Colorado law says that the police are allowed to detain us if they're suspicious for..." She tilted her head as if thinking of the answer.

"I want a lawyer." Sabrina looked at Herczeg. "I'm going to sue you if you keep me here." Then to Lily, "I'm going to sue *you* for my necklace, and for a wrongful death if I find out what happened to..." She gave another delicate sob and covered her face with her hands.

"No one is being detained illegally," the deputy said.

Lily turned to stare at her.

Herczeg sighed and mumbled as if resigned, "A bad storm is coming. We're on lockdown. Traveling is not advised."

The guests turned in unison to look toward the front door. Bright sunlight streamed through the glass.

"There's no storm." Sabrina crossed to the window. The moment she touched the curtain to pull it aside, lightning struck. She jumped back, dropping them. Less than five seconds later, thunder rumbled so loud it shook the house. The outside darkened. The lights flickered.

Polly peeked around the corner from the library. "Looks like a bad one. Guess we should play a board game and wait it out."

Sir, please?

Lily gave a quick look around out of habit but didn't see anything.

Whether Polly made them, or they went on their own accord, Lily couldn't say, but the guests filtered back into the library.

When they were alone in the front hall, Polly said, "We'll have some cosmic answering to do. They'll be more than trees to clean up after this storm passes."

Polly put on a bright smile and skipped into the library. Her cheery voice could be heard ringing out between rumbles of thunder. "Who wants tuna fish salad sandwiches with ketchup and soy sauce?"

"You know this isn't going to end well," Lily whispered. "We're now trapped in here with a killer and a thief."

"And tuna with ketchup and soy sauce, which I think might be the worst of all three." Herczeg frowned. "Isn't there an old board game with this exact same scenario? People trapped in a house looking for a murderer?"

"I don't know. Who has time to play board games?" Lily bit her lip as she thought of the third-floor linen closet. No one used it. She'd seen a few dusty games stored on a top shelf. If she remembered correctly, there was also a spirit board in there. She'd played around on such a board once as a kid with Dante and Jesse, trying to contact their imaginary friend Suellen Grace, but nothing happened. Now that she had powers, maybe it would be different. "I need to take care of some things upstairs."

A loud bang sounded from the back of the house, and she heard her brother say, "Where the hell did that come from?"

Mara and Dante came from the kitchen,

water dripping off them as they shivered.

"Did your magic misfire again?" Mara asked Lily accusingly as she moved toward the stairs.

"Shh," Lily leaned over to look into the library. Mara's footsteps continued upward. The guests sat at two card tables in groups of three.

Polly stood over them, her hands to her side as she said, "Welcome to the game of enchantment, where all your dreams can become a reality! Polly patent pending."

At Lily's concerned look, Polly winked and waved her hands for her to leave. A couple of the guests glanced up at her but appeared calm.

"Now that's what I call babysitting," Dante whispered behind her, as he leaned to look. "Why can't we keep them like that all the time?"

Lily gave him a small elbow jab in the stomach, touching his wet shirt in the process. Though he had a point.

The storm continued to rage outside, sending flashes of light through the windows. The stark contrast of light and shadow gave everyone the brief appearance of monsters.

Lily froze as she vividly remembered such faces, gaunt cheeks and bugged eyes staring in at three terrified children from outside the car windows. Like before, she became a fixture in the memory. Yellow streetlights cast their sickly shadows. Marigold was gone. The paper remains of cheap fast food tacos were wadded on the floor in the corner. They would throw it out in the morning when it was safe to leave the car.

Water trailed down the windows to create a curtain of streaked texture, which wasn't always bad. Storms kept most of the people away and distorted the ugliness of the outside as it cocooned them within their little world.

Dante sat in the driver's seat and Lily in the passenger while Jesse slept in the back. They would try to sleep in shifts, watching over their little sister—at least that's what they'd told themselves. It gave them a purpose and a reason not to give in to their own fears. They would each remain brave for the other.

"What if she doesn't come back?" Dante whispered.

"I won't let anything happen to us," Lily answered. She was the oldest at six, nearly seven. If anything happened to her siblings, Lily knew it would be her fault. "I'll protect us. Whatever it takes, we're staying together. The world can't touch us if we're together."

"Did you find anything out?" Dante asked the deputy, keeping his voice soft. The sound broke Lily from her trance, as he continued, "Which one of them did it?"

"No one broke down and confessed if that's what you're asking," Herczeg said.

Lily took a deep breath, staring at Dante, seeing the image of the boy he'd been in the man before her. Those feelings of protectiveness would never go away. She was responsible. She had to keep her family safe. They needed this to work.

"Lily?" Dante asked, clearly not trapped in the same memory she was.

"I have to get the rooms ready." Lily weakly moved to the stairs.

"Hey," Mara appeared. "Why's someone's stuff in my room?"

"You're with Polly now," Lily answered. Her sense of family responsibility flowed naturally toward Mara, but not as strongly as it did toward the other two.

"But—" Mara tried to protest.

"There's no room, you have to double up," Lily said.

"Ah, come on, seriously?" Mara pouted. "Can't I stay in your room and Nolan can sleep with Dante?"

"Not happening," Dante said.

Lily ignored them and went to look for the spirit board.

Um, sir?

CHAPTER SIX

Nolan's heart pounded as the wind and rain slammed the side of his truck, skidding the tires through the muddy road as it pushed him to the side. The closer he drove toward the bed-and-breakfast, the thicker the storm became. It didn't take a supernatural genius to figure out someone cast a damned spell to keep people from leaving. It was also keeping him from getting home.

He braced himself as the truck flipped over in a gust of wind. It rolled twice, tossing him around the interior before coming to a stop. He hung upside down by his seat belt.

Seconds later, he found time had reset itself and he was driving down the road toward the storm as if the crash had never happened. There was some built-in protection to the spell that kept anyone from getting hurt. That would have been Polly's doing. She was the only one he knew who had such control over her magic.

Nolan pulled his truck over to the side of the road and parked it by a large tree. Branches thrashed overhead, but hopefully the thick trunk would stand and protect the vehicle. The wind blew against him, causing him to stumble.

The safest bet would be to turn around and go back to town. Yet, he couldn't get the thought out of his mind that Lily was trapped in a house with a murderer. Polly might try to protect her, but that was his responsibility. Yes, it was an old-fashioned way to think, as Lily and Tegan were quite capable women. However, the rest of the crew was another story. Mara would think of herself first. Dante loved his sister, but he didn't exactly look like the kind of man to win a fist fight.

Nolan needed to get home.

A ripple of fur enveloped his skin as he pushed the wolf to the surface. His mouth stretched forward and made room for teeth. Strength filled his limbs. The beast represented everything the man suppressed—it was wild abandonment, total rage and hunger, an absolute drive to fulfill the basest of needs. He loved trans-forming into the wild creature, but he hated the destruction the wolf could cause. Only on nights where there was no full moon could he control it.

Running through the woods gave him protection from the wind, but the lightning took out more than a few trees. They lit up in flames only to be put out by the heavy rain seconds later. Even under the protection of overhead branches, the forest floor was mush.

A soft glow caught his attention in the darkness and his shifter senses automatically focused on it. A rabbit stood in a protective bubble, as if unaware of the dangerous storm surrounding it. He slowed his pace at the strange sight and a glowing deer ran across his path, prancing as if it were a beautiful spring day. Dry earth welcomed its steps, only to turn to muck once more as the animal passed.

Yep. This spell had Polly's name all over it. Trust the woman to protect all wildlife with a happy bubble. Where was his bubble? He had his timeline reset every time something almost killed him.

He ran faster. It would also take a great deal of magic to perform. Though he didn't know what the consequence would be for using so much power, he agreed with Lily that there would be costs to this much magic. The universe needed balance.

Lightning struck overhead, sending a loud crack through the forest. He glanced up in time to see the branch seconds before it smacked him on the head. Pain shot through his body as he fell under the weight. For a second, blackness enveloped him, and then he was back on the path, once again running past the same bunny and deer as his journey reset itself.

Dammit, Polly.

At this rate, he'd never make it back.

This time he stopped right before the branch fell so it didn't crash on him a second time. It landed across the path. The thick limb should have killed him the first time it fell. Nolan leapt over the obstacle and kept going. Each second, each step became a challenge. The magical storm did not make his path easy.

The trees thinned as he came closer to the house. Lightning flashed, illuminating the Victorian across the clearing. Nolan paused and took a deep breath as he geared up to run the final stretch home.

Beep. Beep. Beep. Beeeep.

The repetitive honk of a car horn sounded in the distance—three short blasts followed by a long.

He narrowed his shifted eyes trying to see through the thick rain. Lightning flashes lit up the distance. The faintest outline of a car appeared alongside the road.

Nolan looked with longing toward the house. He was so close. The honking paused, only to start up again with more desperation.

Beep. Beep. Beep. Beep.

Someone needed help.

Nolan groaned as he changed direction. He ran against the wind to get to the car. The vehicle had run off the dirt road and was now stuck in a ditch.

Only at the last minute did Nolan force the wolf to hide. The fur receded beneath his skin. Teeth flattened and his claws retracted. Rain pelted his flesh, stinging his weaker human form.

As a man, he was less prepared to deal with the elements. The wind slowed his movements, but he somehow made it to the car. The honking continued. He slapped his palm against the driver-side window to get the person's attention. A man's face turned to him in shock as another flash of lightning sliced through the sky. Dark eyes met his.

Fear turned to relief as the man started to roll down his window. "My car won't—"

"Come on," Nolan yelled over the pounding rain. "There's a house."

"I don't see a house—" the man tried to answer.

"Come on," Nolan ordered. He was freezing, soaked, and didn't feel like having a debate in the storm. "It's just down the road."

The man hesitated and then nodded. He tried reaching for something on the seat next to him.

"Leave it." Nolan wasn't about to carry luggage. It would take all his strength to get the stranger to the house in one piece. Whether he could do that without shifting was another matter.

"But—"

"We'll get it when the storm passes." He looked over the top of the car. The front bumper appeared wedged under a bush and the vehicle was tipped at an angle. "It's not going anywhere."

The man nodded. He pulled his keys from the ignition and got out of the car. Nolan grabbed him by the wrist and tried to guide him to the house. The man struggled to lock his car before letting Nolan lead him. They managed to make it down the long dirt road to the lawn, but it was slow going.

A branch rolled toward them. Nolan acted on instinct. He jerked the man hard and threw his shoulder into his stomach to carry him. He let the wolf partially take over his body, using the animal's strength and hoping the chaos would hide it. The man did not take to the new plan with ease as he struggled to be set down.

Nolan surged on. His muscles burned. Another branch nearly smacked them as it flew from the forest. When they finally neared the porch, Nolan dodged a flying piece of debris when the porch railing broke free.

He tossed his burden at the door. The man stumbled. Nolan tried to get ahold of his shift, but it was difficult to convince the wolf that it was safe to retreat.

In the end, it didn't matter. The man didn't bother to turn around as he fumbled with the doorknob and pushed his way inside.

Lily ran down the stairs. Her widened eyes turned to him in surprise. Then, seeing his shifted gaze, she sprang into action. She gathered the man forward and pushed him toward the library.

"Now." She waved Nolan to go up the stairs. He did, running through the front hall and out of sight.

He stopped at the top of the stairs. Lily pushed the front door shut and latched it. The storm raged on, but inside, the house was still.

"Who's with you?" Lily asked.

Nolan managed to gain control of himself, even as he tried to catch his breath.

Dante came from the third story. Seeing Nolan dripping wet, he arched a brow. "Go for a swim?"

"Something like that," Nolan said.

Lily hurried to join them.

"Who is that guy?" Lily insisted.

"What guy?" Dante asked.

"I don't know. I was trying to get home when the storm hit. I had to leave my truck behind and I ran across that man trapped in his car," Nolan said.

"Dammit, Polly," Lily whispered. "People were not supposed to be hurt. This storm doesn't sound safe at all."

"They won't be. A tree fell on me and time reset itself," Nolan said. "If anything, there will be a lot of confused people to deal with once this passes."

"Polly told me rewinding time wasn't an option. I shouldn't be surprised she lied to me," Lily frowned. To her brother, she said, "You know they're going to blame us for this."

Dante shrugged. "Well, would they be wrong? Polly did start it."

"Maybe Jesse is right. Maybe it's time we cut

our losses and left." Lily ran her hand through her hair. Nolan hated to see her so defeated.

"If that is what you want, say the word," Dante said. "It doesn't matter as long as we're together. Whatever it takes."

Lily nodded. "You're right. The world can't touch us if we're together."

"Wait," Nolan interrupted, not liking where this conversation was going. Didn't he have at least a little bit of a say? Lily was his girlfriend. They were living together. That had to mean something, a commitment to the idea of a future together, at least. "We'll figure this out."

The Goode siblings looked at him, and not for the first time he felt as if they'd put him in his place—on the outside of their sphere looking in. It was a place no one could touch, no one could go, no one could understand. There was only room for Lily, Dante, and Jesse in this world.

Nolan desperately wanted to pull her out of it, into his world, his arms, his future. He worried that if he tried to force more commitment from her, she'd run. That Lily would cut him off faster than he could get down on one knee to propose.

Not that he was about to propose.

That would be ridiculous.

But, someday, he'd like that to be an option.

"Herczeg has nothing," Lily said. "I listened

to her question everyone. It's like a useless pile of stupid stories. Marion was knitting. Frank was snoring. Willy knows nothing. The only thing I'm fairly sure of is that the Elliott kid probably stole Willy's flask, got drunk, and passed out in the backseat of his parents' car. Oh, and that Sabrina is going to sue me. She looks like she can afford a lawyer, so I'm pretty much screwed."

"First," Nolan forced her to meet his gaze, "we don't know that Sabrina is going to sue anyone, but if she does, *we're* screwed. *We're*. Not you. *We're*. We're a team, Lily. We're in this together. I'm not going to leave you holding the bag."

She looked surprised by his words. For a smart, independent woman, she really was dense sometimes.

"Fine, *we're*," she agreed, begrudgingly. "What's the second?"

"Second what?" Nolan asked.

"You said, first we don't know that she'll sue us. What's the second?" Dante answered for his sister.

"Second, the Elliott kid is an idiot and I hope he's hungover," Nolan said for lack of a better second. It was going to be, *I love you and we can get through anything*. But with Dante in the conversation that would have been awkward.

"Third, you're dripping all over my floors. Go dry off before you get sick." Lily pointed toward their bedroom.

"Yes, ma'am." Nolan leaned to kiss her but Dante put his cheek forward.

Nolan swatted Lily's brother away. Dante laughed.

"Where is everyone?" Nolan listened, but the house was quiet. "I thought there'd be a lot more freaking out. You did tell them what happened, right?"

"Yes. Herczeg told them. Polly has them playing board games." Lily sighed. "I guess I should go see what's up with this new guest. I'm not sure where we're going to put him."

"I'll share my room with the hot chick, but I'm not sharing it with a dude," Dante said.

Lily grimaced. "Stop calling women chicks."

Dante gave a devilish grin. "Fine, hot piece of a—"

"I will throw you down these stairs," Lily warned. No one thought she was serious. She'd never hurt her brother.

"What?" Dante tried to act innocent. "I was going to say hot piece of...*ah-avocado*."

"Nice try," Lily muttered. "Can you please clear out of your room? New guy has to go somewhere."

"New guy can go to the couch," Dante suggested.

Lily gave him a pointed look. "If by some miracle we get through this and stay in business, we need every one of them leaving here with something nice to say."

"Where am I supposed to sleep?" Dante asked. "Your floor?"

"Um…" Nolan began to shake his head.

"Maybe Polly can do something with that third-floor storage closet for you," Lily said.

Nolan expected Dante to protest, but the man surprised him.

"Yeah, okay. Slept in worse places." Dante turned to go back upstairs, supposedly to move his belongings.

Nolan started to head back down.

"Where do you think you're going?" Lily stepped in front of him.

"To see who the stranger is and what he's doing out here." He made a move to pass her.

"Herczeg's down there. She'll handle it." Lily gestured that he was to turn around. Her eyes narrowed and she looked around the empty stairwell.

"What can I do to help?" Nolan asked, cupping Lily's cheek now that they were alone. He drew her face around to look at him.

She blinked several times, almost perplexed. Her eyes dipped down over his wet clothes. "Are you all right?"

He nodded.

"Good." Lily gave him a sad smile. "Not that I'm unhappy to see you, but what are you doing going out in that storm? You should have stayed at your house. What if something happened to you?"

"This is my home," Nolan said. "There was no way I was leaving you to deal with all this by yourself."

"I'm not by myself. I have…" Lily bit her lip. "Ah…"

"Precisely. Polly, Dante, and Mara aren't exactly the crisis management dream team." Nolan tried to hug her, but she placed a hand on his chest to stop him.

"Dry clothes," she ordered, turning him by his arm and pushing him into their bedroom. "I want this grand opening over with. When you're done changing, I'm going to need you to tell me everything you know about using a spirit board."

"Wait. What?" He turned to stop her from leaving.

It was too late. She'd closed the door on him.

CHAPTER SEVEN

HELLO, sir? Sir? Please, sir?

Lily cupped her hands over her ears, willing the voice to stop. The words were the loudest they had ever been and their panic filled her as if it were her own.

"Brett Wilson." Herczeg leaned against the doorframe.

"Brett Wilson?" Lily frowned. "Is that who's speaking?"

"Vanessa's ex-boyfriend," Herczeg said, not hearing the voice in Lily's head. "Sabrina mentioned him. He's the guy Nolan found trapped in the car. He claims he was coming here to see her."

Curious, she went to peak into the library. The new guy had a towel around his shoulders and was whispering fervently to Sabrina in the far corner.

"I don't suppose he confessed and we can send everyone home now?" Lily asked.

Herczeg shook her head in denial.

"What do you think of him?" she asked.

"That he works in politics and all politicians are questionable by default in my book," Herczeg said. "Most times, it's someone the victim knows. I also think it's a little suspicious that he happened to be in the area. Who knows if Polly's magical storm stopped him from getting away, or really did just trap him here."

Herczeg pushed away from the doorframe and walked toward the dining room. She glanced back, indicating Lily should follow her. When they were alone, she said, "I can't believe I'm going to ask you this, but do you think you can do the truth spell without Polly? She refuses, and…"

At the deputy's meaningful look, Lily finished, "You want me to try it without telling her."

"Can you?" she asked. "I have no legal reason to keep these people here once the storm passes, and I have no evidence to charge any of them. I'll have no choice but to call in reinforcements."

"Sheriff Tillens?" Lily knew even before she said it that wasn't who Herczeg was talking about. She'd never met the man and had no proof he even existed beyond people saying he was a real person. "FBI?"

"This isn't federal land. They won't investigate unless they get an official invitation from the sheriff. The last time they came through Lucky Valley, supernaturals were almost exposed. No, I'll have to ask for help from townsfolk. Magical help. It could get messy and this won't be kept a secret. The way I see it, you either perform a truth spell or some other kind of spell fast, or I have to report this to the sheriff. The storm bought us some time but—"

Sir, please. I don't like this.

Herczeg kept talking, but Lily couldn't hear the words. Heavy breathing filled her thoughts. Fear trickled through her limbs, causing her hands to shake.

"I'm going to try," Lily blinked hard as she attempted to focus her thoughts, "spirits. I'm going to ask... Spirit board."

Sir, please, sir.

"Spirits?" Herczeg shook her head. "I don't think that's a good idea. The last time spirits were here, Dante let a knocker in and got all gooey-eyed and a ghost army tried to kill you."

"They might know—" Lily began.

Sir?

"Are you all right?" The deputy frowned.

"Um, yeah, yes." Lily nodded. "Just a little headache. Give me a moment."

Even though the voice was in her head, she felt as if it were coming from the kitchen. She went to quiet whoever was doing it. Gnomes were gathered on the dining room floor, huddled in a corner around Herman to create a barrier of pointy hats.

Sir?

The sound still came from the direction of the kitchen. She ignored the gnome convention. As she stepped into the kitchen, the lights flickered. In that instant, the image of the almost finished cottage entered her mind.

Lily rushed toward the door. Rain pelted the wood, drumming violently. She took a deep breath, knowing she would have to make a run for the cottage. Something was out there, calling her. Either they needed to tell her what they wanted, or they needed to shut the hell up.

She unlatched the door and pulled it open.

A blur of movement came at her. She yelped in surprise as she was shoved back into the mudroom. As she stumbled, she caught a fleeting peek at a thick, white mass as it shook and vibrated.

Lily's foot slid on a wet tile and she landed hard on her backside. "*Oomph.*"

Hello, sir, hello, hi, hi, thank you.

The words were panting and breathless. Gratitude washed over her. Lily saw something coming for her and she protectively lifted her arms to cover her face.

Hu-ah, hu-ah, hu-ah...

A whoosh of warm breath accompanied the steady panting.

Lily lowered her arms to find a wrinkled, furry face closer to hers. She pushed up from her awkward position on the mudroom floor.

A fat English bulldog appeared to be smiling at her. He shook off the rain, causing his short white and brindle fur to spike.

Where the heck did a dog come from?

"Hello?" Lily tried to look out the opened back door into the storm. "Is anyone out there?"

Hello, sir, I found you, sir.

Lily blinked as she looked at the dog. Surely not...

"Are you...?" She took a deep breath.

The dog shook again and ambled away from her, running on its squat legs into the house.

"No, wait!" Lily pushed up. She slammed

the door closed and latched it. She followed the wet tracks and the sound of panting through the kitchen to the living room, only to find he was attempting to climb up onto the couch. It took several clumsy attempts, but he finally made it.

"Hey, where'd he come from?" Nolan grinned as he went toward the door. "Aren't you a handsome boy?"

"Friend of yours?" Lily asked.

Nolan arched a brow in her direction as he petted the dog's head. Nothing about the animal appeared aggressive. "It looks like he got trapped out in the storm. We should dry him off and get him something to eat."

The dog flopped onto his stomach, wetting the antique furniture.

Why not? With the day she was having, wet dog furniture was the least of her problems.

"The dog just took Deputy Herczeg's bed, so I don't know how we're going to fit everyone tonight."

"Can I have an old towel? This poor fella is wet." Nolan didn't appear concerned by the sleeping arrangements.

"You can't keep him," Lily stated.

"Oh, why not, he's so cute." Nolan squished the dog's wrinkly face in his hands and shook lightly. The bulldog appeared to like it. "There's something about him."

Lily tried not to smile when the dog looked up at her with a happy expression. His wide mouth pulled up at the sides in an almost ridiculous manner. He *was* pretty adorable.

"What if he belongs to someone?" Lily asked.

"What if he doesn't?" Nolan countered. "He's not wearing tags."

Lily went to get a towel from the kitchen. When she came back, the dog had his head on Nolan's leg and was gazing up at him.

"What should we call you?" Nolan asked. "Buddy? Squishy-face? Mr. Barks?"

Winston, sir.

"Winston," Lily repeated the thought.

"Winston?" Nolan arched a brow. He gave her a slow smile. "All right. Winston. He kind of looks like a Winston."

Lily tossed the towel at Nolan. He caught it before it hit his head.

"Want to magically help me unlock some phones?" Herczeg appeared in the doorway. She glanced questioningly at the dog but didn't comment as Nolan began drying the animal.

"Don't you need a warrant to look at people's phones?" Nolan asked.

"Sure. Let me jump on Polly's flying broom-

stick and go ask Judge Menounos if it's okay."
Herczeg crossed her arms over her chest. "Polly
can't give me an estimate of how long this storm
will last. She said once it's started it has to play
itself out. I need to have some clue before that
happens."

The deputy tried to appear stern, but Lily
could see the exhaustion around her eyes. It
wasn't just tonight, this case, even though that
wasn't helping. It was an older tiredness as if
she'd not had a day off in months and the
stresses just kept piling up.

"Did you take care of the fairies?" Lily asked
Nolan.

"I threw pebbles at the thorns until they
trickled through. When they came out to see
what was happening, I served them with a cita-
tion. I think they thought since I'd retired, they
could get away with a rager," Nolan answered.

Lily glanced at Herczeg to see if that light-
ened her load a little. "And the other stuff?"

"Questionable smells at Cold Hearth Bakery
were coming from a nest a couple of shifter children were making as a clubhouse," Nolan said,
using the towel to pet the dog more than dry
him. "As for the misspelled butt tattoo, I refuse to
investigate the Carter twins' backsides. That's all
you, Deputy."

"Goodie, something to look forward to," Herczeg mumbled. "Can we stop worrying about thorn domes and get to work please?"

"Sure. I'll see if I can unlock those phones for you," Lily said, gesturing to the deputy to lead the way. "Though I can't promise I won't blow them up."

CHAPTER EIGHT

LILY GOODE WAS NOT MADE for solving crimes.

Or magic.

Or dog-sitting.

Or possibly running a bed-and-breakfast.

Lily wasn't sure what her magic did to the phones, but after two seconds in her hands, they stopped working. Every screen froze at the exact same time.

They were running out of options and ideas. Outside, the storm raged on and did not indicate that the rain would be letting up soon. Lily watched it through a third-story window. Lightning flashed, illuminating the grounds. With each flicker of light she tried to see if anything appeared. Even with the protection spells to keep them at bay, there had to be some spirits lingering around the house, ones that had seen what happened, ones that could help them close the investigation.

Polly had all the suspects trapped in a game of Polly's Enchanted Whatever. Lily couldn't guess the rules, but Truckdriver Willy did announce himself to be a pretty princess and did a little dance. It was a sight she could not unsee.

"Hurry," Lily whispered from her post at the door to Polly's room. "Are you sure it's in here?"

"I'm telling you, I saw a book," Mara answered. "It had a ton of spells and potion recipes in it. If there's a way to make people tell the truth, it's in there."

Dante stood at the base of the stairs watching for Polly. His eyes met hers, and Lily held up her hand to gesture that he should keep waiting.

Mara poked her head out of the door and said, "Can I just say, I feel really close to you right now. Nothing like a little burglary for sisterly bonding."

"It's not burglary. It's borrowing." Lily pushed Mara's shoulder so she was forced back into the room. "Find it."

"She moved it," Mara said.

"Keep looking."

"I can't—oh, hey, Herman—*ouch*!" Mara cried out. "What the—the little *effer* pinched me!"

Mara hurried out of the room cradling her hand against her chest.

"What did you do to him?" Lily peeked into the room. Herman sat in the middle of the floor facing them. He didn't move except to open and close a pincher slowly in what looked like a warning.

"Dude, you need to talk to your boyfriend. It smells like wet dog up here." Mara leaned in to sniff her arm.

"Arr-rawr-rar."

Lily and Mara turned toward the sound at the top of the stairs. Winston stood there breathing hard and what could only be called smiling.

"Why do we suddenly have a dog?" Mara sighed. "Isn't this house full enough?"

"You're welcome to leave if you don't like it," Lily offered, irritated by her sister's tone.

"I belong here as much as you do, more even," Mara said. "I don't care what Mom's will said."

There was so much Lily wanted to say, but all of it was mean so she held back. Her anger and frustration were not Mara's fault. All the hard work and emotions since coming to Colorado had begun to take their toll on her. She wanted to cry, scream, fight, hide.

Hide. She wanted to hide, crawl into a closet and never come out.

"Talk to Nolan. He's the one who wants to keep the dog," Lily said.

"He better not hurt the cat," Mara said. "That spiteful little thing is growing on me. Sometimes I think I hear it talking. That, or one of Polly's garden freaks."

"You hear the cat?" Lily glanced down at Winston.

Hello, sir.

The words sounded breathless in her head.

"Maybe." Mara shrugged. "Or I imagined it. Hard to say. If the cat is talking to me, it's grouchy and demanding. Kind of fitting that it's your familiar."

"Omigod," Lily gasped in realization. She'd never felt bonded to the feline. "The cat's not my familiar. It's yours, Mara."

"What? No." Mara shook her head.

"Polly said familiars have bonds. I can't hear the cat, but…" Lily looked at Winston. "I hear him."

Mara started laughing. "Your familiar is a fat dog? That's too funny."

"Hey," Lily felt the need to defend the creature. She wasn't really enthused about having any kind of pet around. There was already too much she was responsible for. "He's not fat. He's kind of cute."

"No, I get it," Mara said. "English Bulldogs are stubborn and willful and...lazy."

"I am not lazy," Lily protested.

Mara eyed her then Winston. "Maybe he's lazy to make up for your being a control freak."

"I'm not a control freak." Lily held up her hand. "I don't have time for this. Any of it. In case you forgot, we have to solve a murder."

"Do we? Why? It's not our job. That's why Deputy Uptight is here."

"Yes. If we don't find out who did it, then everyone will assume it was us. They'll drive us out of here with torches and pitchforks."

"This isn't a bad medieval movie," Mara smirked. "I hardly doubt they'll carry pitchforks. Guns, maybe."

"Someone died." Lily shook her head in disbelief. "Don't you feel a little bad about that?"

"A lot of people have died here." Mara's demeanor became stiff and her expression hardened. "There are over a hundred spirits out there who died in the mines, not to mention the townsfolk also currently residing in Unlucky Valley's spectral plane. We both saw our mother roaming around out there. Sally the knocker has a crush on Dante ever since he let her leak ectoplasm all over him."

Out of all of them, Mara had been the closest to death—literally. Ghosts were her childhood friends, even going so far as to possess her body while she slept. According to Mara, a spirit from Unlucky Valley took possession of a traveler and seduced Marigold. From that gross-sounding union, Mara was conceived. Since the dead weren't supposed to father children, she was what Mara affectionately self-termed a supernatural byproduct.

"Why are you staring at me?" Mara asked defensively. "Mom used to look at me like that right before she accused me of trying to drain the life out of her. I don't like it."

Lily didn't like being compared to their mother. "I'm not her. I don't think you're evil, and I don't think you suck the life out of everything around you because of who your father was. You can no more control that than I can control who our mother was. Marigold damaged herself. You had nothing to do with it."

Lily wasn't one hundred percent sure that was true, but she had to give Mara the benefit of the doubt. The girl did have a spooky connection to the dead, but that didn't make her evil. Just as being dumped curbside in front of an Iowa fire station didn't mean the rest of the siblings were garbage.

"Are you two about done?" Dante called from the stairs. "Did you find it?"

"Does it look like I'm carrying a book of spells?" Lily went to him and held out her arms. As she lifted them, an old book appeared magically in her hands as if summoned.

"Either that or the first edition of *War and Peace*," Dante said, noting the thickness of the volume.

Lily adjusted the book. The brown leather-bound cover was blank. She flipped it open and thumbed through a few of the pages. The pages were handwritten. Some were in a neat, tight cursive, and others meticulously printed in tiny block letters.

Dante came up the stairs and eyed the book. "Did you call forth a serial killer's manifesto?"

"I hope not. It looks like our ancestors wrote this," she answered.

"Yep, that's it," Mara said. "Next time just materialize it. Don't send me in to fight the evil lobster."

As if hearing her talking about him, Herman ran out of the room, his tiny feet tapping as he made a beeline for Mara's ankles. He snapped his pinchers at her. Mara yelped and jumped out of the way.

"Herman, stop teasing her," Lily scolded. The lobster turned its pinchers on her. Winston leapt into action, mouth open wide.

"No, don't eat him!" Lily cried. She lurched after the bulldog, dropping the book.

At the last second, Winston closed his mouth and used his nose to slide the lobster across the floor into Polly's room. Lily grabbed the dog, hugging him close to her. His weight kept her from lifting him off the ground so she stayed on the floor with him.

Food now, sir?

Holding the animal sent a ripple of magic over her. She felt calmer, stronger. "You do know I'm a girl, don't you?"

Yes, sir. Can I have food now, sir?

"Okay, so you have the book. Which are we trying first? Truth spell or spirits?" Dante asked.

"Spirits," Mara answered, rushing toward the small door at the top of the stairs. "I'll set it up."

"I'll help." Dante followed Mara.

Lily loosened her grip on Winston. The dog gazed at her with a dopey look on his large face. She studied his eyes. "Where did you come from?"

The dog licked her hand.

118

She looked across the floor for the family spell book, but it had disappeared.

"Mara says we're ready," Dante said to draw her away from the bulldog.

"Stay out here," Lily ordered Winston. He lay down and stared at the door. "Good boy."

Lily went to the storage room. The soft glow of candles illuminated everything within. The ceiling was high enough for them to stand and the walls were unfinished slats of wood. Nails had once poked through the sides, but she'd made Nolan bend them over with a hammer for safety.

Mara held a container of salt while staring at the white, granular circle she'd made on the floor. A wooden spirit board rested in the middle with a shot glass turned upside down on the surface. It appeared old, with letters and numbers burned into the wood next to the words *yes* and *no* on the surface.

"How do we do this?" Lily placed her hands on her hips and looked around the small space.

"Why are you asking me? I don't use a spirit board to talk to ghosts. They just appear," Mara said.

"Do you see any?" Lily asked.

"Like the last three times you asked, no," Mara answered. "I think we all have to touch the glass, concentrate and just ask. We should sit in the circle for protection."

"And salt works?" Lily stepped over the line. "You're sure?"

"It's a purifier used for blessings and curses," Mara said. "It prevents entities from crossing."

"It's a food seasoning," Dante said. "I feel about as safe as a turkey in an oven."

"You are a turkey," Lily muttered.

"Love you, too, sis." Dante chuckled.

"Are you sure we should let Mara near the Ouija board?" Nolan appeared in the doorway at the same moment Dante was stepping inside the salt circle.

"Spirit board," Mara corrected.

"Ouija board, spirit board, talking board, same thing," Nolan said. "What are you doing with it?"

Lily went to him. "You shouldn't be in here. I don't want you hurt if something goes wrong."

"Lily?" Nolan looked at the séance room and then at her. He didn't move.

"You heard her, wolf boy," Mara added. Nolan frowned at Mara before taking Lily's arm and turning her away from her siblings. The conversation wasn't exactly private, but their body language did not invite an interruption. "Are you sure this is safe? You've been trying to get rid of the spirits. Now you want to invite them back in?"

"We're just going to ask a few questions," Mara said, showing she was actively listening. "No reason to get scared."

Calling upon the dead for help did not seem like a good idea in any situation. Yet, Lily was desperate for answers. "Like Mara said, it's just a few questions."

"If quoting Mara is your best response, then something is seriously wrong," Nolan said.

"Hey!" Mara protested. "I heard that."

"I said it in the same room as you," Nolan answered.

"Enough bickering," Lily ordered. "You can have it out *after* we find out what happened to Vanessa. And I say that to all of us. We can't let stress get the better of us."

"I'm not stressed," Mara mumbled.

Lily arched a brow and looked at her sister. There was so much she wanted to scream at her. In the end, she tried to take her own decree and didn't start a pointless argument.

"I'm not leaving," Nolan said. "This looks dangerous."

While she appreciated his protective qualities, Lily didn't exactly need a man to get all alpha on her. She was quite capable of doing this without his supervision.

Nolan stepped into the circle, sat down, and crossed his legs, indicating he wasn't going anywhere.

"Let's do this," Dante sat across from Nolan. Mara and Lily were slower to join them.

Nolan picked up the shot glass and read the etching on the side. "Lady Penelope's Strip Club?"

"What? I didn't work there. They have great tacos." Mara shrugged. She took the glass from him and set it back down on the board. "I couldn't find the indicator thingy so I grabbed this shot glass."

"It's called a planchette," Nolan supplied.

"Are you some kind of expert?" Lily inquired.

"I'm not, not really, but I have a television. There are a ton of supernatural horror movies being released." Nolan placed his hand on Lily's knee.

"You like horror movies?" Lily asked, surprised.

"Doesn't everyone?" Mara interrupted. "Can we get started or what?"

"We should shut the door." Before Lily could stand back up, the door slammed shut behind them. Lily gave a small jump of surprise at the noise.

"Oops, sorry." Mara grinned. "Everyone put a finger on the glass and focus on getting answers."

They all four reached forward, touching the shot glass with the tip of their finger.

Lily stared at the board, waiting for it to move. One by one the others looked at her.

"What?" Lily whispered, glancing behind her. No one was there. Her finger slipped from the glass.

"Aren't you going to ask any questions?" Mara prompted.

"Oh, um." Lily returned her finger to the shot glass and asked, "Who killed Vanessa?"

She stared at the board, willing it to answer. Nothing happened.

"Maybe start easier. Talk like you would to a person you just met. Ghosts used to be people." Mara cleared her throat, saying louder, "Is anyone with us?"

The makeshift planchette didn't move.

"We would like to speak to someone from the ghostly plain. Is there anyone with us?" Mara asked.

Dante gave a small gasp and whispered, "Did you feel that?"

"No, what?" Lily asked.

Dante looked at her with widened eyes and said in a dramatic voice, "Nothing." His expression changed to one of mocking. "I felt absolutely nothing. This is a waste of time."

Suddenly the glass slid to cover the word *yes* on the board.

"Who did that?" Dante asked.

"Shh, someone's here." Lily waved her free hand to shush her brother before telling Mara, "Ask if they know who killed Vanessa."

Mara arched a brow at the commanding tone. "You're not my boss. You do it."

"Hello. Nice to meet you," Lily said with a roll of her eyes. Why did everything have to be so difficult between all of them? "Thank you for talking to us. Do you know who killed the lady in the back cottage?"

Yes, came the response as the glass slid an inch to the right and then back again to give the answer. One of the candles flickered and went out.

"Can you tell me?"

Yes.

"*Will* you tell me?"

Yes.

"Okay, who?"

There was no answer.

"Dante? Are you messing with us?" Lily sighed.

Dante smirked. "No."

Lily frowned and removed her finger. "Dante, this is serious——"

"It's not me," insisted her brother. He too removed his finger from the glass. Mara and Nolan withdrew their hands. Two more flames flickered out, darkening the room even more.

Suddenly, the glass began gliding under an unseen force, swooshing back and forth forcefully against the wood.

Yes. No. Yes. No. Yes. No...

Lily looked around the room, not seeing an entity but asking it, "Are you trying to say something?"

The shot glass moved slowly over the board spelling out, *Y. E.*

"Great. Now they're spelling yes. I think we got one that's not all there," Dante muttered.

"No, look." Mara pointed.

H. A.

The glass paused.

"What's it trying to say?" Nolan asked. "Y-e-h-a?"

"Yee-haw?" Lily questioned with a frown.

A loud cackle cut the quiet, causing all four of them to jump a little at the hard sound.

Mara laughed. "You got us," she said.

"Dammit, Stan!" Lily yelled at the same time.

Stan Edison was a miner who'd died nearly a century earlier. He'd made it the mission of his afterlife to be a nuisance. The fact Mara appropriated his last name and pretended that he was her father made sense...in a weird way.

"Oe-ee-hee-hee-hee," Stan's disembodied voice chuckled. A slapping sound punctuated his words, but he didn't materialize. "Yer faces!"

"Mara, ask him if he knows," Lily whispered, motioning for her sister to hurry.

"Hey, Stan, do you know who hurt the girl in the cottage? I would mean a lot to Lily if you told us," Mara said. "She'd owe you one."

A low rumble sounded.

"Run!" Stan's shout filled the small room. The transparent, blurred image of a short man with a long, scraggly beard zoomed toward the shut door. Winston barked from the other side, a loud, hollow sound.

A blast of hot air blew against Lily's face, lifting the hair from her shoulders. It carried the smell of rotten eggs, and she gagged.

"Go," Nolan commanded. His eyes shifted as he sprang forward, grabbing her arm to draw her back. Her feet dragged in the salt. They slammed into the wood door.

Rrrrrrr.

The low growl reverberated in the room. All but one of the candles blew out.

Nolan held her tight.

Lily pushed away from him. Her heart pounded and her hands trembled. "Dante?"

"I'm fine." Dante had stepped out of the salt circle and was pressed against the wall. She couldn't see his face in the shadows.

"Nolan, the salt circle," Mara cried, "before it gets out!"

Nolan scrambled down to push the salt they'd scattered back into place to reform the circle. As his arm passed into the center of the ring, something knocked into him. He grunted in pain and fell back.

Mara came around the circle, staying as far away as she could as she joined Dante. She gave him a push. "Hurry. Go."

"What is it?" Dante asked, stumbling toward the door.

The last candle flickered out, casting them in darkness.

Lily pulled the door open. Mara pushed Dante, forcing him out of the room. He fell on the top of the stairs and slid down a few steps. Mara tripped, only to crawl across the third-story floor.

Nolan shoved Lily ahead of him but held her waist to keep her from falling as he slammed the door shut. Lily clutched at the arm holding her. Her fingers slipped in warmth.

Nolan made sure she was safe before releasing her. Lily lifted her fingers to find they were stained with blood. Winston instantly came to her, standing in front of the door with his shoulders squared. He returned the entity's growl.

"Nolan?" She held up her hands to him and then looked at his arm. Three large gashes cut into his skin. Blood trickled down his arm. "You're hurt."

"It's fine." Nolan pulled his t-shirt over his head and wrapped it around the wound.

"What was that thing?" Dante asked.

A growl from the other side of the door answered him. Whatever it was, it now had possession of Dante's new (make that former) third-floor closet bedroom.

"I don't know what we channeled," Mara said, "but it's pissed."

"Great, most people get bats in the attic. We get demons," Dante drawled. His voice lacked its usual languid tone and she could tell he was shaken.

"Nolan?" Lily asked as he examined his arm, flexing and clenching his fingers.

"I'm fine. It didn't get me too badly. The salt thing worked." Nolan nodded toward Mara. "Good thinking."

"Thanks," she said. "But I'm not sure how long it will hold."

"What are the odds this thing will go away on its own?" Lily held Nolan's biceps as she examined his injured forearm for herself.

All three turned to her. Their skeptical expressions said it all. Another low growl sounded, followed by scratching.

"We have to tell Polly what we did, don't we?" Lily's hands shook with fear.

"No, I don't think we'll have to." Dante gestured down the steps. "She probably already knows."

A gnome holding a flower stood halfway up, its statuesque eyes and chubby cheeks appearing somehow accusatory even though they hadn't physically changed.

This was all too much. Everything she tried, failed. Lily felt a tear slip over her cheek and she brushed it aside before anyone could see it. She was supposed to be the strong one. She was supposed to have the answers.

She had no answers.

"Hey." Nolan placed his uninjured arm around her shoulders. "We'll figure this out."

"We can still try the truth spell," Dante said.

The entity kept scratching at the wood floor.

"It's not going to work on everyone, is it?" Mara asked. "I mean, that would be weird, right? If we all started saying everything that popped into our heads."

The woman had a point.

"Got something to hide?" Nolan asked.

"I'm sure we all have thoughts we'd rather not say." Mara frowned. "Maybe we give up. Clearly this isn't working out that great. So far Lily broke everyone's phones, we have a new pet demon, Polly's storm has us trapped with a potential killer. We're not exactly batting a thousand at this point when it comes to solving this crime. Maybe we need to call the professionals."

"Herczeg is here," Dante said.

"Right. Small-town deputy. How could I discount that? I feel so much safer," Mara drawled sarcastically.

"I need to clean this wound," Nolan said, heading toward the bathroom. "Dante, watch that door until I get back."

"Why him? Because girls can't go up against a demon?" Mara asked. Lily couldn't tell if her sister was offended or just being a brat.

"Sure, Mara, go step inside the salt circle and see what happens." Nolan shut himself in the bathroom.

"I'm going downstairs." Mara walked down the steps a little loudly.

"Hey, you all right?" Dante placed his hand on her shoulder.

"I'm tired of the bickering. I know everyone is on edge. I am too. But…" Lily shook her head. "It's fine. I'm just ready for this grand opening nightmare to be over. What the hell was I thinking?"

"That you were taking care of us and giving us a home of our own," he said. "But no house is worth all this. Say the word and we're gone. We'll go home to Jesse, find jobs, and it will be just like it was before."

They knew that wasn't exactly true. This experience had changed them in so many ways. It had not only given them magical powers but a deeper understanding of their mother. Maybe that is all they were supposed to find in Lucky Valley.

She felt the weight of responsibility pulling at her like never before. It was a ball of festering stress and anger that had been tied around her ankle with an exposed nerve. All she had to do was sever it and it would fall away. Sure, what was left would ache and she'd feel the phantom pain like people who'd lost a limb, but it was better than living with gangrene.

"Okay," Lily whispered. She wasn't sure how she would tell Nolan, but she couldn't think about that now. "I'm done. As soon as we can get out of here, we're going back to Washington. Don't say anything. Polly will try to trap us here. If Polly and Mara want this house so badly, let them have it."

CHAPTER NINE

We're going back to Washington. Don't say anything. Polly will try to trap us here. If Polly and Mara want this house so badly, let them have it.

Nolan stared at his bandaged arm, the words he'd overheard echoing in his mind. Lily was leaving Lucky Valley. But, more to the point, she was leaving *him*.

And, what was worse, his name didn't even come up as a consideration in the whispered conversation between Lily and her brother. He knew she was close to her siblings. He accepted that it was a club he'd never be let into, but he thought his love, *their* love for each other, would at least factor into any decision making.

Nolan told himself to wait that she would say something to him, tell him, try to explain. He made a point of standing by her, of talking to her. He gave her opportunity after opportunity to start the conversation. She didn't. She pretended like everything was normal—well, as normal as could be under the strange circumstances.

Polly fed the guests so many snacks that an evening meal wasn't necessary. The drain of keeping seven people enthralled was beginning to take its toll on her, as was evidenced by the slump of her shoulders and the tired lines forming around her eyes. He didn't want to be the one to tell her that they'd summoned a demon upstairs. Luckily it didn't look like he'd have to. Lily had pulled her aunt aside. He could hear the faint trace of their whispers in the living room.

Nolan walked around the library, watching and listening. The game had ended, but not the conversations. Frank and Marion sat beside each other. Their moody son pouted by himself slumped over in a chair. Junior's fingers twitched as if they could still feel his confiscated phone. Nolan wondered how the kid really got his black eye. He highly doubted it was a tree branch like the Elliotts claimed. Lily might think they were boring, but Nolan felt like they were hiding something.

Nolan focused his shifter hearing on eaves-dropping while staring at the spines of the books.

"I'm missing a knitting needle," Marion said to her husband. "Do you think it's outside?"

"If it is, the storm has blown it away. We'll get you a new one when we get home," Frank assured her. There was tension in their voices, but that could easily be explained considering all that was going on.

"It sounds bad out there," Marion whispered. "Do you think we're safe here?"

"House feels sturdy enough," Frank answered.

"If anything happens to my truck..." Willy mumbled to himself as he stared out the window at the storm. "If I don't stop more than fifteen minutes every four hours, I should still be able to make the long haul."

Janice was trying to fall asleep in a chair. She kept swatting at the air next to her head, but he didn't see an insect or anything that might be bothering her. Sabrina huddled in a corner with Brett. He assumed they were commiserating over their lost friend. Sabrina, in particular, acted upset.

Lily appeared in the doorway and glanced in at the guests.

"Your aunt is a genius." Herczeg joined Lily in the front hall. He focused his hearing on them. "I thought she was insane, but there is a method to her madness, clearly. Her crazy game calmed them down, loosened them up, and they're starting to talk."

"You know what to say." Sabrina's voice interrupted Lily's response.

Nolan turned to look at Sabrina. She gripped Brett's arm. They both glanced at the deputy.

Suddenly, Janice stood. Her eyes were half closed. She shook her leg and then collapsed back into the chair.

Junior laughed. "I want what she's on."

"Be nice," Marion scolded.

"I'm bored. Can I go up to the room?" Junior stood as if not waiting for permission to leave.

"Oh, um." Marion looked to her husband for the answer.

Frank looked at the deputy before nodding. "I think that'd be all right."

Junior took off up the staircase.

"No, wait," Lily called.

The footsteps didn't stop.

"Let him go," Polly said.

Nolan rushed to where Lily, Polly, and the deputy talked. Junior might be a brat but that didn't mean they wanted to feed him to the entity in the attic.

"I'll stop him," Nolan said.

"What's going on?" Polly eyed the three of

them like they were naughty children. "What have you been up to?"

Lily averted her gaze. So much for Lily having told her aunt about the demon.

"Lily Camellia Goode?" Polly warned.

"We tried to contact the spirit world to see if they knew anything." Lily dug her toe into the wood floor as if doing so required all of her concentration.

"Is that all?"

"With the spirit board," she answered.

"In this weather? What were you thinking?" Polly lifted her hands to the side and began walking around the living room as if trying to sense something in the air. "You know better than to contact the spirit realm when the east vortex is all *gobbledygooked*.

"I'm going to talk to the guests again," Herczeg said, leaving Lily to be scolded.

"I didn't know that," Lily defended.

"Everyone knows that," Polly quipped. She crouched down.

"What are you doing?" Lily asked.

"Trying to find it before it eats anyone," Polly said. "This is bad. Very bad. Where's Florus? It will definitely want to eat him first."

Lily's widened eyes met his.

"Upstairs," Nolan said. He moved to lead the

way up. "We have it trapped in the storage closet on the third floor. He's guarding the door with Winston."

"Winston?" Polly asked, following him.

"My familiar," Lily said.

"How long was I in the enchanted forest with those people?" Polly asked as they reached the second floor. "I guess my spell to call people to this place is working in unexpected ways. These storms always make magic a little tricky. So what is it? A mole? A turkey? Please tell me it's not a chicken."

"Uh, demon." Lily pointed to the stairs, where Dante waited.

"No, that can't be right. Your familiar wouldn't be a demon." Polly waved her hand in dismissal.

"Florus-eating demon." Lily tried to push past him, but Nolan took the steps two at a time to get there first.

Dante sat on the floor.

"Where's Mara?" Lily asked. "I sent her back up to help you."

"Bathroom," Dante answered. "I think. She said something. I didn't pay attention."

Winston stood in front of the storage room door, body squared as if waiting. Scratching came from inside.

"Well, who is this?" Polly asked, reaching to pet the dog. He gave a small lurch at her touch. Polly snatched her hand back. "Yep. Exactly like Lily before her coffee."

Polly reached for the storage room door and threw it open. Lily inhaled sharply. Winston darted inside. Nolan stopped Lily from surging in after the animal.

Herman came running out of Polly's room.

"Time for battle." Polly scooped up the lobster and then slid him through the open door before waving her hand to force the door to a close. She dusted her hands.

Lily managed to break free of his hold and went to rescue her dog. She tugged at the handle but the door was locked as the evidence of a fight resounded. The entity growled. Winston barked. Things slid and crashed.

"Polly, what did you do?" Lily hit her shoulder violently against the wood.

Dante came to help Nolan pull Lily back. They each grabbed an arm.

She kicked her legs forward. "Let me go!"

"Relax. What did you think familiars are for?" Polly went into her room, completely unconcerned.

Lily calmed down a little but remained stiff

as she stared at the locked door. The noise from within continued.

Polly returned holding a book. "Now, would someone like to explain why you were looking for this?"

"Whoa, what's going on?" Junior came up the stairs. He stopped before reaching the top.

The storage room became eerily quiet.

"What was that?" Junior insisted, his tone accusatory. "Who do you have in there? I knew you guys were freaks." He turned to run. "Dad!"

"And a *bip!*" Polly pointed a finger at the kid, shooting magic at the back of his head. Junior paused mid-action, only to move in extreme slow motion. "I swear. That boy needs some manners. The adults are talking now. Where were we?"

"Winston?" Lily jerked out of Nolan's grasp and tiptoed toward the door. She leaned her ear against the wood. "Winston? Herman?" She pulled away and looked at Polly. "I can't hear them."

"Why would you hear Herman? He's not your familiar." Polly laughed. She threw the book behind her head and it disappeared mid-air. She waved her hand toward the storage room door, thrusting it open.

Nolan followed Lily inside. The light flickered on. The horrible smell that had come with the entity still lingered but wasn't as foul as before. Salt was spread all over the floor in streaks as if something had rolled through the circle. In the middle, Winston lay unmoving. Herman was trapped under one of the dog's large paws, his backside near Winston's head.

"No!" Lily darted forward in a panic.

Winston took a deep breath and let out a loud, rumbling snore. She stopped short of touching him.

"Are they…sleeping?" she asked in surprise.

Nolan looked around the room, but the oppressed feeling was gone. "Where did it go?"

Winston took a deep breath before burping.

"Oh, that's so cute! They're having a slumber party," Polly said in an excited whisper. "Let's leave them be."

Lily felt around in the air. "When you said *they're*, who did you mean?"

"Oh, they ate the demon you foolishly brought through," Polly said. "No need to worry."

"Ate?" Dante asked.

"Of course, they're familiars. What did you think familiars do? They protect us." Polly chuckled and waved her hand in dismissal.

A floorboard thumped from below. Nolan stepped closer to Lily, ready to shield her.

Bartholomew popped his raccoon head up from below. He made a chattering noise as he weaved his way to Winston and Herman. Bartholomew collapsed beside Winston, using the bulldog's side as a pillow. He was instantly asleep.

"All that's missing is Mara's cat," Dante said.

"I heard my name. What's going on? What I miss?" Mara joined them. "And what's with the human popsicle on the stairs?"

"Demon's gone," Dante said.

Mara looked around as if it were no big deal. Nolan knew better. He'd seen the fear on her face when they ran from the demon that had been summoned to this room.

"I don't know if it matters or not, but Stan is downstairs trying to hijack that writer lady's body." Mara scratched the back of her neck. "I thought you'd want to know."

"What?" Lily demanded. "Why didn't you stop him?"

"What was I supposed to do? Make a scene in front of everyone? Yell, *hey, ghost, get out of that lady?*" Mara defended. "I let you know, didn't I? And I did try to wave him over. He ignored me. Willy thought I was flirting with him so if I'm kidnapped later, the trucker did it."

Lily went to the floor to reset the board the raccoon had uprooted. She frowned as she reached into the hole. Nolan went to stand over her and watched what she was doing. She pulled out a sparkly shoe with frayed edges and set it down before sitting on her knees and reaching back in. Next, she found a metal fountain pen, a spatula, his new drill bits, a knitting needle, an earring, several coins, and candy wrappers.

"I guess we know who's been sneaking into the rooms and stealing from the guests," Lily muttered. She frowned at the pile of sleeping animals before leaning closer to the floor. "Anyone have a flashlight?"

"I have my phone," Dante said. "What are you looking for?"

"Flask and necklace. They're the only reported items from the guests that I don't see here." Lily took the phone from her brother and peeked inside. "They're not here."

"Maybe he left them in the walls," Nolan offered.

"Yeah, maybe. Wait…" Lily pulled out a tarnished gold necklace with blue stones. "It's like we discovered a pirate's treasure."

She returned the phone to Dante and held out her hand for Nolan to help her up. "Well, that's one mystery solved."

"Really, Florus," Polly scolded. "You should know better than to steal."

Dante held up his hands. "Hey, why are you all looking at me? I didn't do it."

"It's your familiar," Mara said. "Might as well have been you."

"As the elder, I'll have to ground you for this one," Polly said. "I'll have to remember exactly what it is to ground, but when I do, you're it. Nolan, I have a feeling I'm going to need one of your shovels."

"Sure." Nolan couldn't help himself as he grinned. "How deep do you want the hole?"

Dante shot him a nasty look.

"No, this is good." Lily stood in front of her brother as if to shield the adult male from the rest of them. "One mystery solved. We know it's the raccoon who has been stealing from the guests. We also know the thievery isn't linked to the murder. We should tell Herczeg."

"What are you going to tell her? The raccoon did it?" Mara asked.

"Yes. It's the truth. What is she going to do? Arrest Bartholomew?" Lily slipped the necklace into her pocket and picked the pen and earring out of the pile. Nolan reached down to retrieve his drill bits.

Polly led the way downstairs, pausing by Junior to grab his ear. The second she touched him, he shouted, "Ow, let me go, crazy lady!"

"Come with me, young man," Polly said, walking him down the stairs with her. "We're going to talk to the deputy. I know you're hiding something. No one circumvents the tree of truth in the enchanted forest unless they have something to hide."

CHAPTER TEN

"COUGH IT UP, BOY," Polly demanded. She'd sat Junior down at the dining room table and stood over him with her hands on her hips.

Junior rubbed his ear and glared at Polly.

"I've read your stars and the path ahead of you is murky," Polly warned him. "If you don't come clean, I'm afraid you'll be destined to pick garbage up alongside the road in the hot sun. It will be a very unpleasant weekend. You'll get sunburnt. *And* your friends will find out you like boy bands."

"That's an oddly specific threat," Herczeg muttered in Lily's ear.

"I don't like boy bands," Junior retorted. He crossed his arms over his chest. "I don't know anything."

"Oh, I know something," Polly said, sounding uncharacteristically stern. "You know that I know, don't you? I know the thing. If you talk, Deputy Herczeg will go easy on you. If you don't...well, I'm afraid we'll have to throw the book at you. Either way, the truth is the truth. So, what's it going to be?"

"What?" Junior frowned in confusion. "I want my dad."

"Sorry, you're an adult," Herczeg said. "Answer the questions."

"I don't know what...?" Junior looked around the room at the three women staring back at him.

"How did you get the black eye?" Lily asked.

"Oh, um, ah..." Junior touched his cheek. "Car door?"

"Try again," Polly said.

"That trucker guy hit me," Junior said.

"Willy?" Lily said in surprise.

"Try again," Polly demanded, slamming the flat of her hand on the table.

"He didn't punch me." Junior leaned away from Polly. "He pulled my shirt and I fell and I hit the edge of the door."

Lily tried to picture what the kid said. "Why was Willy pulling your shirt?"

Junior shrugged.

Polly pinched her fingers and aimed at the kid's ear.

He covered his lobe with his hand and ducked his head. "It was the first night he arrived. I'd never been in a truck before. If he didn't want people checking it out, he shouldn't have left it unlocked."

"Did he have the black eye yesterday?" the deputy asked Lily.

Lily shrugged. "I didn't pay attention to the kid yesterday. Maybe?"

Herczeg took a deep breath. She went to the basket where they'd placed the phones. She placed one with a marijuana sticker on the table. "Open your phone."

Lily looked to see if it was still frozen from her magical attempt to break in. It wasn't.

"What? Why?" Junior looked panicked.

"You're eighteen and nearly had a heart attack when I took it from you. If what you say is true, the evidence will be on there in a post or message or whatever it is that's the cool thing this week." Herczeg nudged the phone toward him with her fingertip. "Open it. Prove you weren't with Vanessa and we can all move on."

Junior grabbed the device and held it. "You can't tell my mom, Okay?"

"That you were breaking into a semi?" Lily clarified.

Junior didn't answer as he typed his passcode, 6669. He began pushing buttons. The deputy swiped the device from him. Lily leaned close to watch. Polly put her hands on her hips and stared down at Junior.

Herczeg opened the photos and began scrolling. The first several were of the backseat of the Elliotts' car and some blurry ones taken through the window. It was impossible to see what the pictures were supposed to be. Then there was a picture of the ground and more that were blurred. Next, there were several selfies in the back of the semi-truck, many inappropriate.

"You licked the back of the seat?" Lily grimaced and shook her head at the kid. "Seriously?"

"It's for an online game," Junior defended.

"It's Ebola waiting to happen," she answered.

"You should see what he's doing to your gnomes." The deputy held up the phone. A gnome in a blue hat was taped to the base of a tree with silver duct tape.

"Let me see that?" Polly demanded. She gasped. "Mr. Twittlebum? That's it. Lock him in the slammer!"

"Twittlebum?" Junior smirked.

"What's going on in here?" Marion appeared from the hallway. "Why are you talking to my son?"

"Chill, Mom," Junior dismissed. "They're just asking me if I know anything about that dead girl."

"Her name is Vanessa," Herczeg said. "You might work on showing a little empathy."

"You can't take anything he says the wrong way." Marion rushed to her son's side. "He sounds like that when he's nervous. Come on, Junior. Your dad is waiting for us. Time for bed."

"We know about the black eye," Lily stated. This woman had lied to them earlier. "We know he was in Willy's truck."

"Do you want to tell us what happened? For real this time?" Herczeg gestured that the woman should sit.

Marion hesitated before touching the back of the chair. She started to pull it out, only to stop. "There isn't anything to talk about. We worked everything out with Mr. Willy. He doesn't want to press charges. Did he say he wanted to press charges? Because he assaulted my son if he does and—"

"No one is pressing charges at this time. We just need to verify where everyone was last night. For real."

"What about Mr. Twittlebum?" Polly insisted. "He's out there all alone."

"Who's Mr. Twittlebum?" Marion asked.

The deputy held up Junior's phone.

Marion gasped. "Frank Chester Elliott, you apologize to these nice ladies at once." She pushed at Herczeg's hand to lower the evidence as if that would erase what her son had done. "We, of course, will reimburse you for any damages."

"Poor Mr. Twittlebum," Polly said. "He'll be traumatized."

"We'll work something out," Lily put forth, not caring about the gnome.

"Let's start over." Herczeg held up her hands for silence. "Mrs. Elliott, where were you last night?"

"My son is adventurous. You know how boys are," Marion said.

The deputy crossed her arms over her chest and eyed the woman. Polly mimicked Herczeg's posture.

"He didn't harm anything. Boys will be boys, after all. I think Willy overreacted when he yanked him out of the truck," Marion said.

"Did you see this happen?" the deputy asked.

"Well." Marion stood behind her son and held the back of his chair. "No. They were having a disagreement when I arrived, but we all decided it was just a misunderstanding."

Lily touched Herczeg's arm and pulled her aside. "I believe her. It sounds like Marion was worried her son would get into trouble for trespassing, and Willy was probably trying to hide the fact he'd accidentally knocked Junior with the truck door."

"Agree." Herczeg nodded. To Marion, she said, "You should both get some rest. And no more lying. This is a murder investigation and I could bring you up on charges for obstructing justice, among other things."

"Yes, ma'am," Marion said. She grabbed her son's arm. Junior tried to pick up his phone but his mother swatted at his hand, forcing him to leave the device behind.

"I'll bring in Willy," Polly said. "This time I want to play good cop. Lily, you be the bad cop. Tegan, you just be a cop. They're tired now. I think we can wear the truth out of them."

"They're tired?" Lily scoffed under her breath. She collapsed into a chair. "I feel like I've been awake for a week."

Herczeg rubbed her eyes. "I've been averaging three hours of sleep a night."

"How do you do it?"

"Coffee. Lots of coffee. I've been trying to

153

convince the sheriff that we need help. He keeps saying he's looking and then disappears for another week." Herczeg yawned. "Forget I said that. I shouldn't have said anything. I don't want it to get back that I was complaining. I need this job."

Lily nodded. "Already forgotten."

"I'm not sure I can be of help," Willy said as Polly led him into the room. "I already told you that I don't know anything about the poor girl. We didn't cross paths. You're welcome to search my room."

"I have," Herczeg said.

Mara rushed in behind them. "Uh, Lily?" She pointed over her shoulder, only to gesture at her to hurry.

Lily stood up from the chair.

"I guess you're free to go," Polly said with a hard slap on Willy's back. "Have a good night, sir. Be sure to tell all your friends how much you love the Garden Gnome Bed-and-Breakfast!"

Willy looked confused.

"Wait, no," Herczeg interrupted. "No one is leaving just yet."

Lily brushed past him to follow Mara, who was waving frantically. Mara moved toward the library and pointed.

Janice walked stiff-legged toward a bookshelf.

Sabrina and Brett sat on the other side of the room, watching her. Janice's arm flung and her hand moved as if it had trouble judging distance.

"I think she had a stroke or something," Sabrina said. "She's been flopping around like that."

Lily shared a look with Mara. Her sister shrugged.

"Janice?" Lily asked, venturing closer.

The woman's eyes were partially closed and she had a dopey look on her face.

Lily motioned at Sabrina and Brett to leave the room. "The deputy would like to speak to you both before you go up to bed."

She had no way of knowing if that was true, but if Stan was using Janice as a puppet suit, they didn't need the socialites watching them exorcize him. When they left, she touched Janice's shoulder and asked, "Janice, can you hear me?"

Janice dragged her hand over the top of a couple of books and they fell onto the floor. She reached into the bookcase and pulled out a flask.

"Stan!" Lily demanded under her breath. Janice's head turned at the sound. Lily frowned and studied the woman's dazed eyes. "Get out of her at once."

Janice lifted the flask to her mouth. Lily slapped it out of her hand.

Mara touched the woman's shoulder and jerked her arm back. The transparent image of Stan came flying out from inside Janice.

"Hey!" Stan protested.

Janice wobbled on her feet and held her head. "Whoa, I don't feel so well."

"I think you should go lay down," Lily said. "It's been a long night."

Janice blinked as if she didn't know where she was. She looked around and then nodded before stumbling her way to the stairs.

Mara held her hand out in the air, pinching Stan's shoulder. The old miner looked eternally dusty in his old clothes and hat. His unkempt beard was stained. Lily didn't understand how her sister was able to hold on to the spirit but assumed it had something to do with her heritage.

"All I wanted was a little taste," Stan protested. "The big fella has the good stuff."

Lily picked up the flask. The smell of hard liquor was unmistakable. Some had sloshed out of the loose cap. She touched the shelf where it had been hidden and was thankful that the wood was dry.

"I was jus' borrowin' her." Stan tried to wiggle out of Mara's grasp. "She don't mind."

"Were you borrowing her the last couple of nights?" Lily asked.

Stan stopped struggling.

"Answer and I'll forget you were possessing Mrs. Foster." Lily wanted the grand opening to be over. In fact, she wanted the entire failed business experience to be over. She felt the burn of tears trying to make their way to her eyes and held them back.

"Stan?" Mara asked. "You don't have to help her, but help me. Do you know who hurt the woman in the cottage?"

"The others aren't happy with you, Mara," Stan said, sounding uncharacteristically serious. "You've blocked them from the house."

Mara averted her gaze.

"It wasn't Mara's decision," Lily said. "It was mine."

Mara glanced up in surprise and gave her the barest of smiles.

"She's easy to borrow," Stan said.

"So last night?" Mara asked.

Stan nodded.

"And I assume you are the reason this went missing." Lily lifted the stolen flask.

Stan nodded again. Mara's grip must have loosened because Stan cackled and slipped away, disappearing into the wall.

Mara dusted her hands. "Janice is cleared. There is no way she had anything to do with it while Stan was joyriding. Not that we thought it was her. She's a flake."

Lily nodded.

If Janice was on an unintentional bender with Stan, then that did indeed clear her. The ghost didn't have the best coordination. Herczeg had agreed it probably wasn't Marion, and the entire Elliott family hardly seemed the type. Willy had been napping most of the evening in the library and it looked like he'd been occupied with Junior's nonsense. Brett and Sabrina showed up after. There was some possibility that they had arrived early to commit the crime, though it didn't make sense as to why they would come back the next day.

Thinking back, the only real reason they thought the killer was staying at the house was because of something Polly had said. Lily knew she should be relieved that it was beginning to look like a killer wasn't there, but that meant this mystery would not be solved in one night. The news would spread and her B&B would be known as a murder house.

"I think the storm is letting up," Mara observed. "Polly said it would do that when we were closer to the truth."

"It's late. Let's get some sleep. I just want to erase this day off the timeline." Lily yawned. "Herczeg will have to stay with you and Polly. I think all the guests have a place to sleep, but if not, can you ask Polly to do whatever she has to? I'm beyond caring at this point. And can you take this flask and give it back to Willy? Tell him we found it on the bookshelf."

"Sure. I can do that." Mara awkwardly patted her shoulder before taking the flask and leaving to find Polly and Willy.

Lily hurried up the stairs to the bedroom she shared with Nolan. The stairwell lights flickered as thunder crashed. She heard a cackle before Stan yelled "yee-haw" while sweeping past the top of the stairs. Lily felt a cold chill from his passing but didn't react.

Her feet shuffled as she went into her room. Nolan was sitting at the end of the bed. He'd kicked off his shoes. Tired eyes met hers.

"You look beat," he said.

"I could say the same about you." Lily crossed toward him and wrapped her arms around his shoulders, holding him to her chest as she stood before him. "I'm glad you're here."

He returned her embrace.

"I wish I could go to bed and wake up anywhere else," she said.

"Like Spokane?" His arms dropped away.

"Well, yeah, maybe." When he didn't hug her again, she stepped back.

"Were you planning on telling me that you're leaving?" Nolan asked.

"What are you talking about?"

"I heard what you said to your brother." Nolan pointed at his ear. "Shifter hearing, remember."

"What did I say to…?" Lily frowned before remembering the conversation. "Oh, that."

"You said you were going to go back to Spokane and let Mara and Polly keep this house. You're planning on leaving. You told him not to tell anyone, but I heard you." Nolan eyed his hands as he laced his fingers together.

Lily reached for his face, cupping his cheeks to force him to look at her. "I would never leave you without saying goodbye."

"So you *are* leaving," he concluded.

"Dante and I talk about running away from our problems a lot. I don't expect you to understand. You were raised in a house with walls and scheduled meals and…" She tried to smile, hating the look in his eyes. Even though she hadn't meant to, she knew she had put the hurt there. "It's just a thing we do. Sometimes, we might even think we mean what we say, but it never lasts."

"I'm never going to fit into your world, am I?" Nolan pulled her hands away from his face. "You and Dante live in this secret place and there is no room for anyone in it but Jesse."

"I don't expect you to understand," she repeated, trying to think of a way to explain. Her nerves were frayed and the words wouldn't come as she liked.

"You mentioned that already." Nolan stood and she took a step back to put space between them. Lily grabbed his hand and held tight.

"I don't expect you to understand what it was like to be Marigold's children." Lily closed her eyes. Images from the past hit her and she was back in the car. She felt the uncertainty building inside her, but she didn't have time to process the feelings. She had to push it down into the pit of her stomach and lock it away.

She saw Jesse's tiny face, still streaked with tears. The toddler had fallen asleep hungry and lay across the backseat. Dante sat behind the wheel, his finger lazily moving around the giant circle, round and round and round. His features were gaunt. They'd been sharing their food with Jesse to make sure their baby sister had enough.

Lily's stomach growled. "The streets look

empty now. Lock the door behind me. I'm going to find something for us to eat."

"Don't leave us." Dante's small hand grabbed her arm and squeezed.

"I'll never leave you. When we get out of this hellhole, and we will get out, we'll go together. I promise," Lily answered. "Guard Jesse. I think there was a restaurant down the street. They should be closed now. I'll be back as fast as I can."

Lily jerked herself out of the memory. She blinked to refocus her eyes as she regained her bearings.

Nolan stared at her hand on him. "Was that real?"

"What?" Lily glanced behind her. The door was still open.

"The car."

Lily released him and drew back. "You saw that?"

"And felt it," he said. "Why didn't you tell me?"

"I did. I told you we lived in the car." Lily went to the dresser and pulled out a long t-shirt and leggings.

"You made it sound like you spent a few nights in the car," he said. "That wasn't just sleeping in the car. You were abandoned, starving."

Lily shrugged, trying to downplay it. This was not something she would have talked about, given a choice. Damn her uncontrollable magic.

"So what happened? Did you find food?" Nolan went to close the door.

"Uh, sure, probably." Lily pulled out of her jeans. "We're alive, aren't we?"

"You can't hide yourself from me." Nolan came close to her back. "I felt what you felt."

She pulled on the leggings. "No. I didn't find food that night. I tried breaking into a Chinese restaurant. The owner was sleeping inside. He chased me off, and I spent the night hiding behind a dumpster. Dante was completely freaked out the next morning because I didn't come back right away. Marigold showed up with a bag of French fries and a jug of orange drink the next afternoon, none the wiser and acting as if everything she did was normal."

"I'm sorry that happened." He gently pulled her around to look at him.

"This is why I don't talk about it. I don't need your pity." She took a deep breath, knowing she was being mean. Nolan didn't deserve that. "But thank you."

"I'm here if you want to talk about it," he said.

"I know." She nodded. "I still wish that *we* could go to bed and wake up anywhere else."

"We?"

"Yeah, we." She gave him a small smile. "I know I'm all over the place and none of this is what you bargained for when you moved in with me."

"I didn't bargain for anything," he assured her. "I moved in because it felt right. I'm here because I care about you. None of what is happening is your fault. You didn't hurt Vanessa."

Lily closed her eyes. "Nolan, I just want—"

A knock sounded on the door. Lily sighed as Nolan turned to answer it.

"Hey." Dante pushed his way in. Her brother carried a blanket and pillow. He dropped the pillow and spread out the blanket on the floor by the foot of the bed.

"What are you doing?" Nolan arched a brow.

Dante lay down. "I'm going to sleep. This house is full up."

Nolan looked at her, and she shrugged before crawling into bed.

"Can you get the light, Nolan?" she asked.

Nolan closed the door and flipped the light

switch. She heard him moving around in the dark. Lightning flashed and she saw the outline of him taking sweatpants from the dresser. A minute later, he slid into bed next to her. His hand slipped over hers.

Anywhere but here, she thought as she fell asleep.

CHAPTER ELEVEN

"THIS DOESN'T LOOK VERY ROMANTIC." A woman's voice came on a whisper.

"It doesn't look very comfortable," another added.

"This doesn't look very sanitary," came a louder, wry-toned response.

"Should we call the sheriff?" a man asked.

"Should we poke them?" inquired yet another woman. Or was it the same one? Lily couldn't tell anymore as the voices kept talking.

"Is that...*her?*"

"Heavens to Betsy, don't wake her. We should go. Margie, come on, we're leaving."

Bells jingled.

"I'm going to call the sheriff," the man stated.

When it became apparent it wasn't a dream,

Lily wrenched open an eye. She blinked to adjust to the bright light. The bed beneath her was hard and her pillow was missing. The ceiling was covered with shiny silver. Her gaze focused on a chewed piece of gum stuck to the bottom of a table.

Gross.

Movement blocked her view as Nolan sat up. He gave a quick glance around before turning to look at her.

"I'm going to venture a guess, but I think you transported us to breakfast." He glanced at her shirt and grinned.

"No." Lily groaned as she sat up. They were on the floor of Stammerin' Eddie's, the local Lucky Valley diner.

The comforter from their bed had transported with them, but the mattress had not. Nolan stood and reached to help her up. The black-and-white checkered tiles were cold and a little dusty as she stood barefoot.

A crowd of patrons had gathered around and were staring at them, including the group she secretly referred to as the Santa mafia. The five men looked like the big guy with their graying beards and robust figures.

Okay, they looked like Mr. Claus if Christmas had been canceled and Mrs. Claus ran off with

Rudolf the Reindeer. There was nothing jolly about them, and the few times she'd interacted with them, all they did was complain and look at her like she was the one who'd introduced Rudolf to their wives.

A man with black hair frowned as he took a woman by her arm and escorted her to the closest booth. The woman stared at them openly. Others followed the couple, moving to seat themselves.

Sally, the only waitress Lily had ever seen working there (besides Edna, who owned the diner with her husband), pushed her way through the Santas. Her auburn hair was pulled into a bun on the top of her head, decorated with her black rectangular glasses. She slid her glasses down her face, took one look at Lily and Nolan, and then sighed. "It's too early for this nonsense."

"Is that supposed to be you, Nolan?" One of the Santas pointed at her shirt, causing the others to laugh.

Lily glanced down. She'd bought the night-shirt out of a discount bin for fifty cents. It featured a puppy with rainbow fur and read "Puppy Love" across the chest with cutesy hearts. It was the last thing she'd wear in public—especially in front of *this* public.

"My three-year-old niece has the same shirt," another Santa added.

Lily pulled at the hem before grabbing the comforter and wrapping it around her shoulders like a shield. She started walking toward the front door.

"Hell of a storm last night. Took out my mailbox." A man in a red flannel cap entered and brushed past her. He sat at one of the barstools in front of the food prep area. The serving window gave off a red glow. "Coffee, Sal."

"You got it, Paul," Sally said. "Fresh pot coming up."

"While we're here, might as well get breakfast." Nolan hooked her by the arm and turned her toward the rectangular dining room floor lined with red booths.

"What's wrong with the machine?" Paul asked.

Lily glanced back to see Sally putting "out of order" notes on the soft serve ice cream machine and milkshake blenders.

Sally gave Lily an accusatory look. "Just a precaution."

Lily ignored the booth Nolan picked in the middle of the room and went to the back of the restaurant, away from everyone. He got up and joined her, taking the seat across from her.

"That milkshake explosion was not my fault," she said.

"I know." Nolan nodded.

"Why would my magic bring us here?"

"I don't know. Maybe it wanted scrambled eggs and bacon." He gave her a small smile and reached to take her hands in his.

"I said I wanted to go anywhere," she muttered, staring at one of the tin signs on the wall trying to sell some defunct brand of 1950s cooking oil. "I'm sure there is a nice ice tundra that would give me a warmer welcome than these people."

"Give it time. Once they get to know you, they'll love you. Just like I do." He kept holding her hands.

"Hopefully not just like you do," she whispered, unable to help the small laugh that escaped her. Seeing everyone staring at them, she leaned forward. "Seriously, we need a ride back to the house."

"We'll hitch a ride with the sheriff. Herb called him." Nolan grabbed a menu and handed it to her.

"I thought that guy was just threatening and

being a jerk," Lily said. "We didn't hurt anything."

"He was, but Herb never jokes about calling the sheriff. He has him on speed dial." Nolan's eyes darted to where the man with dark hair sat.

"I don't suppose you have your phone?" She set the menu down, not looking at it. Sally began moving around the diner with a coffee pot.

"Did you see that storm last night?" Sally said to a table at large. When she received the obvious answers, she added, "I don't know about you, but to me it seemed a little sudden. As if caused by supernatural forces." Again, Sally glanced in Lily's direction.

"Don't usually sleep with my phone." Nolan picked up the menu and opened it before giving it back to her. "Don't usually sleep with pants on either, so I count myself lucky there."

"I don't want eggs. I want coffee." Lily glanced at Sally, who was making the round to every table but theirs with a coffee pot. Louder, she said, "And if I don't get coffee soon, I'm ordering a milkshake."

Sally huffed as she came toward them.

Lily turned over the two ceramic cups that were part of the table settings so they could be filled.

"Thanks." Nolan reached for sugar. "Edna here?"

"She'll be in around noon today," Sally said. "Eddie's on the grill, though, so what can I get for you?"

Lily saw a cowboy hat pass by the front window. The man wore a faded brown leather jacket over a dark green button-down.

"Nothing, just the coffee." Lily watched as the man came through the front door. A badge had been pinned to a belt loop on his denim jeans. Thick work gloves covered his hands. She waited for the steady clop of cowboy boots and was surprised to see he wore black sneakers instead. "Is that…?"

"Morning, Sheriff," one of the Santa's called.

"Morning, fellas," the sheriff answered as he took his hat from his head. His overgrown, graying brown hair had a ring where the hat had resided. He paused at the table to exchange old-man pleasantries with the grumpy Santas.

"Yep, Sheriff Franco Tillens," Nolan said.

The sheriff's years were etched in the lines around his eyes and mouth. Gray new growth peppered his face. He looked just as she'd imagined, like a man who didn't smile because he didn't have to, and who lived his life astride a horse in the wilderness.

"I can't believe he's a real person," Lily whispered, watching the man. "I suspected you all made him up since he was always off fishing and Herczeg is always working."

Nolan's lip curled up at the side as he lifted his coffee to hide his amused expression behind the cup.

"Fishing is a code we use for outsiders, Miss Goode," Tillens stated loudly without looking in her direction. "We can't very well say I'm sealing portals and watching for demon hordes. Though I can see how you'd think rescuing ladies after they'd been treed by a couple of bored teenagers is more important."

His tone didn't change, but the sarcasm was unmistakable. The other patrons did not hide their amusement at his statement.

"That happened once," Lily grumbled. In her defense, the two boys had shifted into wolf and cat form and chased her like she'd been their next meal. "I didn't mean to imply you weren't doing your job."

"Yes, you did." Tillens nodded once to the Santas before approaching Lily and Nolan.

The sheriff stood over them, and she had the distinct impression of being a child in trouble with the principal. He eyed the two of them.

"Well, are you going to sit there, or are we going to go catch a murderer?" he asked.

"How...?" Lily gasped in shock. She stood, hoping that would prompt him to lower his voice. The comforter was still wrapped around her. "How did you hear about that?"

"Dr. Cole sent me the autopsy report." His voice did not lower. "I was on my way out when I got Herb's call that I needed to arrest the Goode witch for camping without a permit on the diner floor."

"You need a permit to camp on the diner floor? There is such a thing?" Lily averted her gaze. She was wrong. He didn't make her feel like a student in trouble. He made her feel like she was on America's most wanted list. "And we weren't camping. It was a mistake."

"I'm not arresting you for camping," the sheriff said.

"Oh." Lily sighed in relief.

"It would have been breaking and entering," he added.

"No. I mean, we were in here, but we didn't break anything or enter...the...door." Lily felt his eyes on her.

"Lily, I think Sheriff Tillens is teasing you," Nolan said.

"Not much of a sense of humor on this one,

is there?" The sheriff's tone had not changed once during the exchange.

"Would you mind giving us a lift back to the bed-and-breakfast since you're heading in that direction?" Nolan asked.

"Come on." The sheriff strode from the diner. He slapped his hat against his leg a few times as he moved, before slipping it back onto his head.

"Allow me." Nolan came close and swept her up into his arms, comforter and all.

"What are you doing?" she protested in surprise.

He walked with her out of the diner, not appearing to care about the stares they received. "You're barefoot."

"So are you," she countered, not fighting his embrace.

"Yeah, but I'm willing to risk the dirty side-walk for you." Nolan gave a small laugh.

"So romantic," she whispered.

"I have my moments."

Lily caught the door before it closed behind the sheriff and pushed it open so they could go through. Tillens strode in front of them toward an old SUV. The sheriff department's star emblazed the side. It was dented in as if someone had kicked it. Nolan walked her to the passenger side and waited for her to open the door before setting her inside. He got into the backseat behind her.

The sheriff said nothing as he started the vehicle and pulled into the street. A long banner hung over Main Street advertising an Annual Wilderness Festival. Small animals were drawn across the bottom, moving from trees to a creek in the mountains.

Two women in denim overalls were busy hanging smaller matching banners on the light poles. One slipped as she climbed on the ladder and fell down a few rungs. Lily stiffened as they both turned to look at the passing SUV. Both women saw her, and she knew she'd be blamed for the bad luck of falling off a ladder. Lily slouched in her seat and ducked her head.

"Seat belt," the sheriff said.

Lily buckled her seat belt.

"Dead woman in a cottage on Goode property. Can't say I'm surprised. Not the best of luck." Sheriff Tillens stepped on the gas, speeding as they neared the edge of town. "Any trouble with her ghost?"

"No," Nolan answered.

"Earthquakes or sinkholes?" the sheriff asked.

"No," Nolan said.

177

"Any sign of gremlins?"

"No."

Lily lifted her head to peek out of the window as they spoke. Seeing the street was empty, she sat up straighter. She pulled at the edges of the comforter.

"Good, good." Tillens nodded to himself. "When I heard the victim was strangled, I thought maybe they'd found a way to breach the cave. And the storm?" He glanced at Lily. "That your doing?"

Lily gave a small shake of her head.

"Polly," Nolan said. "To contain the guests to give Herczeg time to interview them before they tried to leave town."

"Polly Crawford?" Tillens straightened a little in his seat. "She still here? I figured she'd be off on her next adventure. Last I heard she was living in Maine."

By his expression, she couldn't tell if he thought that was a good or bad thing.

"She decided to stay and help me with the bed-and-breakfast," Lily said.

"She still with Herman?" he asked.

"Yeah, he's here," Nolan answered.

The sheriff became quiet. He dodged debris in the road left from the storm. Puddles splashed, fanning out from the tires. Lily braced her hand on the dashboard as they bumped over a particularly rough patch of the dirt road.

Tire ruts led off the side of the road to Nolan's truck parked next to the trees.

Nolan leaned forward. "Hey, can you stop? I want to pick up my truck."

The sheriff hit the brakes and the SUV skidded in the mud.

"Thanks, I'll follow you back." Nolan opened the door.

"But, you're barefoot." Lily turned around in her seat, eyes wide, as she silently begged him not to leave her alone with the sheriff.

"I think your puppy will be fine," the sheriff said.

It took Lily a moment to realize he was poking fun at her nightshirt. Nolan chuckled and hopped out of the car.

With some maneuvering, he managed to get his truck back on the road. She watched him from the side-view mirror, aware of the uncomfortable silence in the SUV. The outline of Nolan's head was shadowed in the truck and she wished she was next to him. She tried to bring up her magic to make it happen, but the sheriff's words interrupted her attempt.

"So what are your intentions? It's obvious you're not grounded."

"Grounded?"

"Lack roots."

"Oh." Lily stiffened. She opened her mouth to answer, but a strange noise came out before she managed a stunted response. "They're, ah, good. I care—*of course I care*—but it's too soon to make intentions. I just got here. I mean, it's working for now. These things take time. I'm not... I love him."

"Him?"

"Nolan." She willed her magic to transport her. Even if she ended up under the truck at this point, it would be more comfortable than being interrogated about her relationship.

"Why would I care about your intentions with Nolan?" The man shook his head as if she were crazy.

"Well...you asked?"

"The town. What are your intentions with the town?" the sheriff clarified.

"I inherited a house and I live here now because of it," Lily answered. "My intention is to *live here* and run a bed-and-breakfast. Well, it *was* to live here and run the bed-and-breakfast, but now I might make chocolates or something. Having guests at the house has not been working out like I planned."

"Mm-hmm."

"I know the town blames me for the bad luck, but I swear I'm not doing anything to cause it. I have nothing against the town or the people in it. Well, Sal's a little grouchy, and she keeps telling everyone I blew up the milkshake maker, which I didn't, but I don't have a score to settle."

"If you say so."

Lily turned to stare at him. "I do say so. I want to make a home where my siblings feel safe. Jesse doesn't live with me—yet. I'm trying to get her here from Spokane."

Lily wondered why she was telling him that. It was none of his business.

"Mara lives with me, though," she continued, as if her mouth couldn't stop, "which I still find odd, considering I didn't even know about her until like a month ago. I haven't forgiven my mother for leaving us behind. I tried. Then to know I had a baby sister I never knew about... well, I can see why Jesse wants to steer clear of all of this mess. Sometimes, I think she's right and I should pack up and run away."

"So your intention is not to live here," he inserted.

"No, it is. I mean, it probably is. I want it to work, but..." She frowned, feeling stress weighing on her as they neared the driveway in front of the house. "That poor woman. I feel responsible. If I didn't open this place, she wouldn't have been here, and she'd still be alive."

"Your logic is faulty." Tillens turned into the drive but had to stop when a large tree blocked the way. She heard Nolan pull up beside them.

"How so? This happened on my watch. I'm responsible." As Lily said the words, she knew they were true. She'd been blaming herself, and that guilt was eating at her. It made her try to control everything around her, to make the people stay, to try to solve the mystery. She had told herself it was to protect her business from more rumors, but in truth, she was embarrassed. She should have known something terrible was going to happen. She'd mentally gone through all the contingencies before inviting guests into her home, or so she'd thought.

"Did you kill her?" He turned off the engine.

"No. I would never."

"Then it is not your fault. It's that simple. And you don't know that she wouldn't have died if she'd been anywhere else because you don't know *why* she died." His words carried the same even tone she was quickly associating with him. He nodded toward her window. "Your ride is here."

Lily turned to find Nolan opening her door. She pulled off her seat belt.

"Want a lift?" He turned his back to her.

"I'm probably too old for a piggyback ride," Lily said, even as she moved to climb on. If he were offering to save her from sludging through mud barefoot, she'd be foolish to not take him up on the offer.

When they moved away from the sheriff, she whispered, "You could have warned me the sheriff has the supernatural power to make people confess when he asks questions."

"I didn't know he could," Nolan said.

"I can't. This girl of yours talks a lot." Tillens strode past them.

"He does have excellent hearing though," Nolan noted.

"That I do." The sheriff went up the front steps. He tapped beneath his earlobe. "Thanks to modern science and the miracle of hearing aids."

Nolan set her down on the steps. "I'm going to rinse the mud off my feet with the hose. I won't be but a moment."

Lily nodded and tucked the comforter around her shoulders before following the sheriff into the house. She saw the curtain by the front window shift to reveal Dante's face. Her brother rushed to her when they walked through the front door.

"Where did you go? Who's this?" Dante asked.

"Sheriff?" Herczeg quickly set a pastry down on a table in the front hall. She dusted off her hands. "I didn't know you were coming out."

Tillens sighed and glanced around the front hall as people began to gather. The Elliotts came from the living room. Willy walked down the stairs. Mara and Polly entered from the kitchen.

"Catch me up." The sheriff grabbed the deputy's pastry and handed it back to her as he made his way toward the dining room. He glanced back when others would follow. "Give us a moment, folks."

Polly stepped in front of the sheriff and crossed her arms. "I've been deputized. Where do you want me, sir?"

"Who would do a fool thing like that?" The sheriff shook his head and pulled off his hat. "I un-deputize you. Wait here."

Polly gave a small gasp and clicked her tongue. "Someday soon, Sheriff, you're going to need a ride down to funky town and my taxi service is going to be closed."

"Duly noted," the sheriff answered.

Lily moved toward her aunt. "Funky town?"

"Mineshaft. Old air smells funky," Polly said.

"Of course." Lily quirked a brow. "Let him go spelunking on his own. That'll teach him."

"Sugar bee, did you hit your head? You're talking gibberish again." Polly patted her arm. "Wait here. I'll go get your breakfast."

"Dammit, Polly," the sheriff grumbled when her aunt entered the dining room.

"Don't you grouch at me, you old flirt. It's not my fault you can't get the nerve to ask me out on a date. No reason to act like a schoolboy. You're too old and I'm too much of a catch." Polly came back carrying a tray of pastries, calling behind her, "And you need to watch your cholesterol. Eat the oatmeal."

"Polly, I don't think he's trying to ask you out on a date," Lily said. "He's here on police business. Maybe we should let him work."

Polly touched her cheek. "Don't you worry. I ordered candles. They'll be here soon."

CHAPTER TWELVE

"Did she finally get rid of the creepy gnomes?" Sabrina asked Brett as she sauntered down the stairs in front of him. "Definitely a good choice."

Lily stopped on her way out of her bedroom, stepping back to hide from them. She'd changed her clothes and had pulled her hair into a messy bun on the top of her head. A cold chill swept past her and she closed her eyes.

"Vanessa, if that's you, I'm sorry. We're trying to find out what happened to you." Lily listened to the quiet room. No spirits from beyond answered her. Sometimes a chill was just a chill.

What was the good of having all these powers if she couldn't do anything useful with them?

A *thunk-thunk thunk-thunk* sound came from outside the room. Winston poked his wrinkled face into the door and smiled—either that, or he was panting heavily from his walk and it looked like a smile. He waddled his way over to the bedding Dante had left on the floor and flopped down. Seconds later he began to snore, which was strange because he had one eye open, looking at her.

Lily took a deep breath and went downstairs. Winston stayed where he was.

Sabrina was right. The gnomes were nowhere to be seen. She found it odd, but hardly worth worrying about.

The sheriff had pulled off his gloves and was shaking Willy's hand. "I think we've taken enough of your time, sir. You're free to go just as soon as Nolan gets the debris out from behind your truck." The sheriff released his hand.

Willy gave her a partial smile before rushing up the stairs. Relief was evident in his steps.

"Are you sure?" Lily asked the sheriff. "I don't know if Herczeg had a chance to tell you, but that man has a temper."

"He jerked a teenager who was trespassing out of his rig," the sheriff said. "He may be a truck driver, and that kind of ramblin' man scares some folks, but it doesn't mean he's a murderer. Man's truck is his livelihood. I'd have done the same thing. In fact, I didn't read anger in him at all. He seems the type of man to send money to his widowed daughter every month to help support his two grandkids."

"How could you know that? He didn't say anything to me about having a family." Lily looked up the stairs where Willy had disappeared.

"You don't strike me as the type to ask people questions about their lives," he answered.

Janice came from the library. "Is it true we can leave now?"

"Oh, um, Sheriff Tillens?" Lily glanced between the two. "This is Janice…um."

"Foster. Janice Foster," the writer answered.

"Ma'am." The sheriff reached out his hand. Janice hesitated before taking it. He locked his eyes with hers. "Nice to meet you."

Janice tried to pull her hand back, but the sheriff held on to it a few moments longer.

"Yes, you can go. Be sure to leave all your towels. New business like this can't afford to go missing them," he said.

Janice pulled her hand away and gave Lily a guilty look. "Of course. I—"

"Oh, wait." Lily reached into her back pocket. "We found this pen in the living room by

189

the couch. I think it might be the one you're looking for."

"Why, yes!" Janice grabbed it even as she backed away from them to the stairs. "Thank you. I really appreciate everything you've done here. I mean your hospitality." Her heels hit the steps. "Sorry about that poor girl. I hope you figure out who did it."

Lily's gaze followed the woman until she was out of sight. "I can't believe she was going to steal my towels. How did you know that?"

"There is a reason why people call the authorities when bad things happened. We're trained to deal with them." He crossed to the window and pulled back the curtains.

"I called the deputy," she said.

"And then begged her to keep this quiet. I don't blame you. You're not the most popular family in town. Still, you're lucky Dr. Cole reached out before you all made a bigger mess of this case than you already have. That storm you kicked up probably blew away any evidence that was lying around."

"I didn't think of that," Lily admitted. No. She'd been thinking of protecting her family's future.

"And what if the person who did it wasn't

here?" he asked. "What if this storm helped the killer get away?"

"We wanted to…" Lily averted her gaze. The man had a disappointed air about him.

"Your aunt is careless with magic," he stated. "This storm was a bad idea. I hope that in the future you won't fall too heavily under her influence."

She gave a small frown. "Where is Polly?"

Lily listened but couldn't hear her aunt.

"I sent her out back with your brother after I spoke with them," he said. "It's better if they're out of the way right now. I don't need them pulling any more stunts."

"What about Mara?"

"Your sister is hiding from me. I'll deal with her later," he said. "For now, is there anything else you're not telling me?"

"We summoned a demon but the bulldog and lobster ate him," Lily answered.

"Of course they did." If she wasn't mistaken, he cracked the smallest of smiles.

She watched his mouth. No, she was mistaken. There was no smile.

"Let's get on with this, shall we?"

Lily stepped out of his way when he would go into the library, only to follow him. The gnomes were still nowhere to be seen.

"You must be Frank Jr." The sheriff moved straight for the young kid sitting on a chair. He reached into his pocket. "I believe this belongs to you."

Junior stood as the man approached him and stumbled back in trepidation. Tillens pulled out Junior's phone and handed it to him.

"You spend too much time on this thing," the sheriff said.

Junior swiped it from him and mumbled something as he stared at the floor.

The sheriff placed a hand on the teenager's shoulder. "Speak up when you talk so people can hear you and look them in the eye."

"Thanks," Junior answered, tugging his arm away with a glance up.

The sheriff studied him for a moment before saying, "You're welcome."

Junior made a beeline out of the library.

"Something off about that kid," the sheriff said.

"He's a moody teenager whose parents let him get away with being a brat," Lily answered.

"You may be right." Tillens strode from the room. "Never was one for dealing with kids. They don't seem to take to me."

"Surprising," Lily muttered wryly before thinking better of it.

He arched a brow.

"I mean, you're clearly a fun guy. I've seen you smile like never this morning."

At that, he chuckled. "I find it advisable to refrain from grinning while solving murders."

"Point taken," Lily said.

Nolan came from outside. He instantly smiled at her but said to the sheriff, "I'm working on what you asked. Trucker and Janice can get their vehicles out. Going to be a bit longer on Brett, Sabrina, and the Elliotts though."

"Why don't you take a break? I need to have a few conversations." Tillens looked in the living room. It was empty.

"Do you want me to show you the cottage?" Lily asked.

"No." Tillens shook his head. Voices from the dining room seemed to draw him forward.

"Hey, what happened to all the gnomes?" Nolan asked her. He pulled her arm and planted a quick kiss on her mouth. "You look beautiful, by the way."

"I have no clue," she answered. She tapped his damp shirt. "And you look sweaty."

"Ms. Lily, Mr. Nolan." Willy carried a duffle bag as he came down. "I saw from my window that it looks like I can get my truck out. I'm going to be taking off now. I have a lot of miles to catch up on or I'll miss out on my next job."

"Thank you for staying with us. I'm sorry it was…" Lily wasn't sure how to finish that sentence.

"It was different, to be sure." He nodded even as he reached for the door.

"Do you want a receipt?" she asked.

"No, I trust you." Willy didn't shut the door behind him as he hurried toward his rig. Within moments, he was negotiating his way out of the drive.

"Don't think he'll be back anytime soon," Nolan said.

"That's good because we don't have any more rooms to rent," Lily answered. "I'll figure something else out for money, but I'm done in the hospitality business."

Nolan sighed and slowly nodded. "Whatever you want."

Lily wasn't sure what she'd done to deserve such a supportive boyfriend, but she felt guilty for the doubts she'd been having. "When this is over…"

"Yeah, we'll talk." Nolan tilted his head and held up his hand for silence. "The sheriff is speaking with Brett and Sabrina." He grabbed her arm and led her toward the dining room.

They paused by the door where the others couldn't see them.

"...not here for Vanessa, were you?" the sheriff was saying.

"Yes. I was," Brett said. "I was coming here to meet her."

"I thought you said *you* were coming here to meet her, Miss Hills," Tillens said.

"I was," Sabrina answered.

"But you weren't together?" the sheriff clarified.

"No, my plans changed last minute," Sabrina said.

"And I was surprising her," Brett added.

"There was no reason for the two of us to come here together," Sabrina insisted. "We're not friends."

"Not really. We see each other at parties," Brett said.

"Just parties," Sabrina added.

Lily shared a look with Nolan. There was something hurried about their tones.

"So the affair is new?" Tillens' voice kept the same even tone it always had, almost as if he were tired and just going through the motions.

"Affair?" Sabrina gave a loud gasp. "Whatever do you mean?"

"So your relationship is not new?" the sheriff asked.

"We're not in a relationship," Brett said. "Sabrina and I only know each other through Vanessa."

"And parties," the sheriff said.

"Yeah, parties," Sabrina answered.

Lily couldn't help herself. She leaned to peek inside the room. Herczeg stood silently in the corner watching her boss work. Sabrina fidgeted. Brett stood with his hands on his hips.

"Aren't you supposed to be finding Vanessa's killer?" Sabrina demanded. Her eyes darted to Lily, catching her spying.

"Sit down, young lady," Tillens ordered. "You too, son. The deputy is going to keep an eye on you while I search your rooms, your cars, your bags, and whatever else I can find."

"You can't do that without a warrant," Brett protested.

"You're impeding an investigation," he said. "Lying to me wasn't a good idea."

"But…" Sabrina protested. "Brett…?"

"Sit," Tillens commanded. They both obeyed.

Sabrina leaned away from Brett, turning her back slightly toward him.

Tillens gestured his hand when he saw Lily. "Show me where they're staying."

Lily nodded. Nolan let them go first before following them upstairs.

"Sabrina is on the second floor and Brett is on the third," Lily said. "What makes you think they're together?"

"I'm guessing the lipstick on his neck isn't his shade," Tillens answered. "He tried to rub it off, but the iridescence is still there and on his fingertips."

"People do weird things when they are grieving," Lily said. She nodded toward Sabrina's room. "She's staying in there."

"Possibly, but my gut says they're guilty of something." The sheriff went to where Lily pointed.

Nolan stayed quiet.

"Vanessa stayed on the third floor." Lily gestured toward the floor above. "She had already checked out, so I thought it would be all right to put Willy in that room. I didn't see anything out of the ordinary when I cleaned it. This was before we knew anything had happened. With the storm, we were limited on where we could put people, so Brett ended up in Dante's room."

"I'll take it from here." The sheriff closed the

door to keep Lily and Nolan from following him inside.

"So, do you think Sabrina and Brett hurt Vanessa because they were having an affair?" Lily frowned. "It seems obvious. I can't believe I didn't see it before."

"I think the problem will be proving it," Nolan said. "Maybe Polly can force a confession?"

"She still doesn't want to use truth potions," Lily said. "She says it's too messy and after my last idea to summon a spirit, I'm not sure I trust myself to try it without her. Though, really, it would have made this whole experience much easier."

"But now that we know who we need the truth out of, maybe it'll be easier." Nolan cupped her cheek.

Janice appeared with her suitcase. She nodded once and pointed behind her. "I left my towels on the floor."

"Thanks for staying," Lily managed. "Please leave a kind review."

Janice gave her an odd look before hurrying down the stairs.

"Please leave a kind review?" Nolan questioned.

"We need reviews," Lily defended. "And what

else was I supposed to say? Thanks for not stealing our towels?"

Nolan gave a small laugh. "Do I take it we're staying open?"

"I don't know. My mind changes every three seconds. Though, I do know I'm not made for police work," Lily said. "On movies they make it look so easy, but it's probably because all the clues are laid out and we think we're so clever, following them around. But in real life? It's a mess. There's no script saying you should look at the friend and boyfriend 'cause they're cheaters."

"I think there might be crime investigator handbooks or training. There are psychological reasons why they look at family and friends first in investigations."

"I'm really happy that I'm not a detective," Lily said. The sound of Sheriff Tillens rummaging around the room came through the door. "I have a hard time figuring out what I should do, let alone what everyone else is doing."

Nolan pressed his forehead to hers. "We're going to get through today. That's all we have to do. Get through today. Tomorrow, we will figure out everything else. Let the sheriff do his job. No one said you have to solve crimes."

"Nolan, I don't know what I'm doing. What if I can't make this place work? What if—"

"Shh. Tomorrow. We'll worry about tomorrow, tomorrow."

"You're right." She nodded. "We'll get through today."

"Is the driveway clear?" Frank Elliott appeared with two packed bags. "I heard the other guests say we were leaving. I'd like to take my family home now."

"Almost, we're working on it," Lily said.

Marion joined her husband. She too carried a bag.

"We'll go ahead and check out now. I'm going to load our luggage into the car. Please let me know what the final bill is." Frank glanced at his wife as they moved toward the stairs.

"Oh, wait." Lily patted her back pocket, feeling for the stolen earring from Bartholomew's stash. "Is this the earring you were looking for?"

"Ear…?" Marion touched her earlobe before nodding. "Oh, yes, thank you."

The sheriff came from Sabrina's room as Lily handed the diamond toward Mrs. Elliott.

"Let me see that." Tillens intercepted the jewelry, plucking it from Lily's hand before Marion could. He held it up and rolled it between his fingers.

"It's just a lost earring," Lily said. "I found it in the living room couch."

"Like the pen," the sheriff mused as if to himself.

"A lot of things get swallowed up by that couch," Nolan lied.

Lily hoped the sheriff didn't ask too many more questions. Even though Dante had nothing to do with the raccoon stealing from the guests, she couldn't help but feel that, in protecting Bartholomew, she was protecting her brother.

"Looks fancy. Where I grew up, a man only buys his wife these things on special occasions or if he did something wrong," Tillens said. She wasn't sure if it was his attempt at a joke.

"I suppose," Frank said.

"Our twentieth wedding anniversary," Marion inserted. "They were a surprise."

"No." Tillens continued to stare into the stone.

"No?" Marion repeated.

Tillens handed over the diamond. "It can't be easy having a husband who cheats on you."

"Mom?" Junior asked from the stairs.

Frank's mouth opened and closed. No sound came out.

Lily stared at him in surprise. Boring Frank stepped out on his wife? She would have never guessed.

"Let's go," Marion said. She pushed at Frank's arm. "We're leaving."

"Some say it's a weakness, cheating," the sheriff continued. "I tend to agree. Only a weak man would go back on his word. Are you a weak man, Frank?"

"I think we've been more than patient, but it's time for us to go," Marion said through her clenched teeth as she nudged her husband to go down the steps. "Come on, Junior. Get in the car."

Junior went after his parents. Their footsteps were hurried as they made it to the bottom level.

"Is their car still blocked in?" Tillens asked.

"Yes," Nolan said.

Tillens moved to go after them. "Hold on. I need to ask you a few questions."

"We already answered the deputy," Marion denied.

"I'm the sheriff," Tillens said, "and I need to ask you a few more questions."

Lily followed Nolan down the stairs.

A blur of movement caught her attention seconds before a piece of luggage made contact with the sheriff's chest. He stumbled back, knocking against Nolan and Lily, and they all three fell like dominos. She landed on the wooden stairs with an *oomph* as the wind was knocked out of her. Nolan fell to her side as if trying to avoid landing on her.

"Run!" Marion yelled.

"Stop!" the sheriff ordered.

"Are you all right?" Nolan asked her.

Activity erupted all around. The sheriff pulled himself up and moved to chase the Elliott family. The front door slammed open. Sabrina called out. Herczeg dashed from the dining room to run outside.

Nolan held his hand out to stop Lily from getting up. "Wait here."

The sound of a car's engine revved. Shouted commands seemed to go unanswered.

Lily wanted to see what was happening. Her limbs tingled as magic surged through her. She tried to stop it but the force was too powerful. One second she was trying to push up from the stairs, the next, her feet were sinking into the mud.

Lily stood in the driveway watching the house. Tires spun as the Elliotts' car skidded toward the porch in an effort to get out of the driveway. The storm had blown the railing off the porch so that it barely hung on as it laid on the ground. Mud splattered the sheriff and deputy. Frank drove over the railing and side-swiped the wooden porch before he kept going.

The car turned, leaving deep ruts in the ground.

It happened fast. By the time Lily realized the car was coming for her and reacted, her muddy feet made it hard to leap out of the way, and she stumbled. Frank's eyes met hers and widened in surprise. He'd not expected to see her blocking his path. His hands turned the wheel.

The car did not completely obey.

Lily screamed, pushing her hands forward as if it could stop the vehicle from hitting her. Someone tackled her from the side, dislodging her feet from the mud. Their bodies flew before landing on the drive. A combination of pebbles and mud rubbed against her skin as they slid. When they finally stopped, her eyes met Nolan's shifted ones. He'd turned into wolf form to save her, but the animal now faded from his features. He instantly wrapped her in his arms and pulled her close as he cradled her against him.

A loud pop and crunch marked the end of the Elliotts' escape attempt. Lily pushed her head up from Nolan's chest to see that Frank had driven his car onto the lawn before hitting a tree. One of the tires was too close for comfort to where they laid on the ground. White smoke came up from the bent hood.

Mud smeared the length of her right side. It

stained her clothes and adhered the material of her shirt to her body. Her heart still pounded from her close encounter with the car.

"Sugar bee," Polly called from the porch. She stood with Brett and Sabrina. "You shouldn't stand in front of cars like that. It's not safe."

Lily sighed. "Thanks for the tip, Aunt Polly!"

"You're welcome," Polly yelled back.

Sheriff Tillens and Deputy Herczeg circled the Elliotts' car. The driver's-side door was jammed shut. Tillens jerked open the passenger door and Herczeg hauled Marion out of the vehicle.

"Get out," Tillens ordered Frank.

Frank slowly emerged.

"Are you injured?" the sheriff asked Junior. Lily saw the terrified kid shake his head in denial through the mud-splattered window.

Tillens grabbed Frank's arm as he came out of the car and turned him around to press him against the vehicle. He held the man by the back of his neck to keep him pinned into place.

"So…Frank killed Vanessa?" Lily took an automatic step toward from the crashed vehicle. Herczeg stood with Marion near the bumper. "I don't—"

"No," Tillens said, releasing the man's neck.

"Frank *didn't* kill Vanessa?" Lily shared a

confused look with Nolan as he followed her. Her porch was wrecked and the yard was torn up. "Then what's with the joyride through the mud?"

Something in the back window of the vehicle caught her attention. A gnome laid tipped over on his side. Silver tape hung jagged from his blue hat. Bits of tree bark stuck to the exposed adhesive.

"Mr. Twittlebum," Lily whispered to Nolan, nodding at the gnome Junior had tied to the tree.

The sheriff went to where Herczeg held Marion. Lily reached for his arm to get his attention so she could point out the gnome. The only reason Twittlebum would be in the car is if he'd wanted revenge. Well, as much as a statue could want revenge, or whatever force it was that propelled the statues into movement.

CHAPTER THIRTEEN

Tillens grabbed Marion's hand and a surge instantly rushed from the sheriff into Lily. Her entire body stiffened and she couldn't move. It felt just like when she was thrown back into the memory of living in the car, only this time she was floating in the cottage like a speck of dust turning in the air. She couldn't move as her vision passed over the ceiling of the cottage.

"I won't tell her, bird man." A woman chuckled, a sultry sound. "It's your lucky day, to be honest. My boyfriend cheats on me, and the only way to make it cosmically right is to cheat on him before we get back together. It's either you, the trucker, or the layabout Dante. I wanted the construction guy, but he avoids me. Dante will get attached. The trucker is, well…just no. So that leaves you—married men always go back to their families."

Her body rotated and she saw Vanessa standing near the construction pile with Frank Elliott. The man looked nervous but was definitely interested in the proposition she was selling. Vanessa pulled at his shirt and planted a kiss on his mouth. Frank grabbed her by the arms, returning the kiss.

"Frank, are you in here?" Marion threw open the door. The sound of her shout caused her husband to thrust Vanessa away from him. "Junior's in trouble again. He was caught in the back of the…"

Marion stared at the scene before her.

"It's not what it looks like. I was helping her…" Frank's attempt at a lie was about as transparent as a sheet of plastic wrap. "She tricked me into coming in here."

Marion screamed and leapt toward Vanessa. The pile of construction timbers tripped the other woman and Vanessa landed on her back behind them, with Marion on top of her.

Though Lily couldn't see the actual deed, she watched Marion's stiff arms and shaking body.

"Marion, I'm sorry," Frank cried. "Don't!"

Vanessa kicked several times before finally her legs fell slack. Lily's body turned again, and she saw the sparkle of a diamond earring on the boards.

"Marion!"

The shout faded and Lily gasped as she jerked her hand away from the sheriff. She stood on the lawn sweating and breathing hard. Everyone looked as if only a second had passed.

Tillens removed his hand from Marion and reached to pull his gloves out of his pockets. He whispered in Herczeg's ear. The deputy nodded.

"What's going on?" Brett yelled from the broken porch.

The sheriff then whispered something to Nolan.

"Charge Mr. and Mrs. Elliott," Tillens announced to Herczeg so everyone could hear. "I'm going fishing."

"Mom?" Junior cried out. Frank held him back.

The deputy nodded. Nolan went to Herczeg's truck and pulled out plastic cable ties. He handed one to the deputy so she could cuff her prisoner. Marion looked stunned but didn't fight the arrest.

"Mr. Elliott, I'm going to need you to turn around," Nolan said.

Frank hesitated. "What about my son?"

"He's an adult so he can't ride with us,"

Herczeg said. "I'm sure someone will give him a ride to the station."

Sheriff Tillens tried to walk toward his truck. Lily jogged after him. "Wait. What was that? How did you…" Lily looked at his hands. "It's the touch, isn't it? You see things when you touch people."

"Not everyone and not everything," the sheriff answered softly, keeping his back to everyone else, "but even that is too much. I don't want their memories living inside of me any more than you want to be back living inside that car."

"So that's why you stay in the wilderness?" Lily asked.

"Do you know what history rocks show me? Sitting in a field. And fish? Gliding through the water." He glanced back as Brett shouted.

"Is that who killed her?" Brett jumped from the porch.

Sabrina wailed, making a show of fanning herself. Polly pointed her finger at the woman and instantly Sabrina began to cough, her voice becoming inaudible.

Nolan ran to catch Brett before he reached the deputy.

"You got a reading off the earring, didn't you? You knew where Bartholomew found it.

Those were the smudged footprints I saw in the dust." Lily turned to the sheriff for confirmation but he was already climbing into this SUV. He nodded once at her as he turned on the engine.

Dante and Mara came from behind the house. Mara went to stand by Polly as Dante hurried toward Lily.

Dante looked her over. "Are you all right? What happened?"

"Marion caught Frank with Vanessa and she went crazy," Lily answered.

"The Elliotts? Really?" Dante eyed the situation. "But they're so...dull."

"Where were you? Why are you all sweaty?" Lily asked.

"Sheriff made us check the perimeter of the woods. He told Mara we needed to look for anything suspicious. We ran back when we heard the crash."

"The sheriff told me that Mara was hiding from him." Lily glanced questioningly to where Mara was standing slightly behind Polly.

"So he didn't send us to...? You mean I didn't have to traipse around the muddy wilderness?" Dante closed his eyes and sighed. "Figures she made it up. I'll bet she didn't want to hide out alone."

"I'm taking your parents to the Lucky Valley

station," Herczeg told Frank Jr. "You can follow me if you like, but it's going to be awhile before you can talk to them."

"Marion, don't say anything, I'm going to find us a lawyer," Frank said to his wife.

Marion looked defeated and didn't answer as the deputy put her into the truck.

"You got this?" Nolan asked, putting Frank into the vehicle next to his wife. He snapped the seat belt over the man as Herczeg buckled Marion.

Herczeg nodded. "Yeah, the sheriff said I could shoot them if they give me any trouble."

Marion's eyes widened.

"Polly, a little help?" Nolan yelled as he jogged to her aunt. He pointed at the truck. She nodded and waved her hand. Thankfully, no sparkles shot out of her fingertips.

Nolan came back to stand by Lily and her brother. "I asked Polly to freeze them until Herczeg can get them to the sheriff's office. They won't be giving her any trouble."

"One hell of an opening week, sis," Dante said.

Lily gave a halfhearted smile. "We never did things easy in this family, did we?"

Nolan slipped an arm over her shoulders. "What do you need from me?"

"Your keys?" Lily held out her hand.

"They're in my truck," he answered.

"Dante, can you take Nolan's truck and give Junior a ride to the sheriff's office? I want that family gone," Lily said.

"Me?" Dante asked in surprise.

Lily nodded.

"Uh, sure." Dante moved toward Frank Jr.

"I can take him," Nolan said.

Herczeg lifted her fingers in a small wave as she drove past them.

"No, you do a lot around here already. It's time everyone else started pitching in a little more," Lily said. "Junior's harmless. My brother can handle him. He had nothing to do with his parents' crime. Dante will be fine."

Nolan nodded.

"Hey, Dante," Lily called. "Stop by Taylor Towing and see if Colt can come by and get this car out of here."

Dante looked slightly annoyed but waved his hand that he'd heard her.

"I kind of feel bad for Junior," Nolan said.

"Yeah, me too." Lily turned to Nolan, wrapping her arms around his neck. A weight felt as if it lifted off her stomach, like waking from a nightmare.

"Hey, look, the gnomes are back." Nolan

nodded toward the house. Indeed she could see the hats of a few of them poking out from the shrubberies.

"Why don't you go clean up? I'll get Brett's car out of the ditch so he and Sabrina can be on their way." He slid his finger against her cheek, picking mud from her features. "Tonight we can go over what we plan to do about the damage."

"How about…?" Lily refused to release him. "I'll help you get Brett and Sabrina out of here, and then you will come upstairs and get cleaned up with me?"

"Yeah?" Nolan grinned, leaning in for a kiss. "I think that could work."

"Sugar bee, I think you'll want to look at this," Polly called, interrupting them. "The porch is all wibble-wobbled and the house isn't pleased."

Lily finally released Nolan. "I should go deal with that. We wouldn't want the house to be upset."

Brett and Sabrina were inside when she joined Polly and Mara on the porch.

"We need to fix this before the new guests arrive. It doesn't make a good impression," Polly insisted. "That spell I sent out for business worked. New guests should be arriving either in an hour or in nine hours, seven minutes, fifteen seconds. I can't be sure which, but I guess we'll find out soon enough."

"Please tell me they're humans and not trolls." Lily called to Polly. She almost didn't want to know. In fact, she wasn't sure she could handle more guests. She glanced at Nolan. At least, not on her own.

"Human," Polly answered with a shake of her head. "But we need to work on your prejudice against trolls. They're not all bone-crushing man-eaters. Some write interesting songs."

"So does this mean we're still in the B&B business?" Nolan asked Lily.

She gave him a small smile. "It would appear so."

"I'm glad to hear it. I'll get to work on the porch just as soon as we're done with the vehicles," he said.

"Polly, is there any chance you can feed everyone tonight?" Lily asked. "Nolan and I have a lot of cleaning up to do."

Polly grinned. "Think nothing of it, sugar bee. I'll whip up a twelve-course meal! I'm thinking dumplings, nachos, foot-long hot dogs, strawberry pie, spaghetti, corn on the cob, tacos, clam chowder—"

"Sounds like it'll go together perfectly," Lily lied. "Don't forget the pepperoni pizza."

Polly wrinkled her nose and patted Lily's arm. "You leave the meals to me. Proper meal plans are more art than craft."

"We are leaving," Sabrina announced, carrying her own bags. Brett was with her.

Lily retrieved the stolen necklace from her pocket and smashed it into the mud before tossing it beside Sabrina's jeep door.

"Let me help." Lily pulled open the back of the jeep.

Nolan took the bags from the woman and tossed them inside before moving to pull a tree branch away from the vehicle.

Lily reached down to pick up the necklace. "Does this belong to you?"

Sabrina eyed it before pinching it between two fingers. "My necklace."

She tossed it into the back of the jeep with her suitcase.

It didn't take long before Sabrina was heading down the road. Minutes later, they had Brett pushed out of the ditch and on his way.

"Not even a thank you," Nolan said. "Though considering the circumstances, I can't say I blame him."

"I bet you five bucks they leave us a couple of one-star reviews." Lily threaded her arm through Nolan's.

"That's okay. Apparently, we have more people on the way. There has to be a couple of five-stars in the next batch." Nolan pulled her close. The mud stuck their clothing together.

"I hope you don't take offense to this, but you're taking way too long on those back cottages. I think we need to take Polly up on her offer to use magic to finish them. I want to put Dante in one. Mara in the other. Also, when we rebuild the barn, I want to figure out a way to turn it into an apartment. I know we have to keep the old structure plans, but I want to modernize it. We are not staying in that house any longer than we have to. Polly likes people. She can sleep in the house."

"Privacy." Nolan grinned. "I like this plan."

"And, if Jesse decides to move, we'll give her a cottage," Lily said. "Or they can share the house and we'll rent the cottages. I don't care."

Nolan pressed his mouth to hers, stopping her flow of ideas. "Whatever you want, Lily."

Lily pulled back and gazed into his eyes. "I'm always dictating, aren't I? What do *you* want?"

"You." He kissed her again, holding her close. In the distance, she heard Polly and Mara bickering about garden gnomes. Lily glanced to the side, not taking her mouth from Nolan's. Seeing the front door open, she lifted her fingers and magically forced it to shut. It slammed a little too hard.

Nolan turned at the noise.

"Oops." Lily laughed. "I guess I still need to work on my magic."

The End

KEEP READING!

Magick, Mischief, & Kilts!

If you enjoyed this book by Michelle M. Pillow, check out the magically mischievous, modern-day Scottish, paranormal romance series:

Warlocks MacGregor®
Love Potions
Spellbound
Stirring Up Trouble
Cauldrons and Confession
Spirits and Spells
Kises and Curses
More Coming Soon

MichellePillow.com

WANT MORE OF THE LOVABLE POLLY?

She appeared in these Happily Everlasting Series Books:

Fooled Around and Spelled in Love &
Curses and Cupcakes by Michelle M. Pillow

Once Hunted, Twice Shy &
Total Eclipse of The Hunt by Mandy M. Roth

Want more cozy mysteries from Michelle M. Pillow?

Sign up for her newsletter today so you don't miss out on (Un)Lucky Valley books!

NEWSLETTER

To stay informed about when a new book in the series installments is released, sign up for updates:

Sign up for Michelle's Newsletter
michellepillow.com/author-updates

ABOUT MICHELLE M. PILLOW

New York Times & *USA TODAY*
Bestselling Author

Michelle loves to travel and try new things, whether it's a paranormal investigation of an old Vaudeville Theatre or climbing Mayan temples in Belize. She believes life is an adventure fueled by copious amounts of coffee.

Newly relocated to the American South, Michelle is involved in various film and documentary projects with her talented director husband. She is mom to a fantastic artist. And she's managed by a dog and cat who make sure she's meeting her deadlines.

For the most part she can be found wearing pajama pants and working in her office. There may or may not be dancing. It's all part of the creative process.

Come say hello! Michelle loves talking with readers on social media!

www.MichellePillow.com

facebook.com/AuthorMichellePillow

twitter.com/michellepillow

instagram.com/michellempillow

bookbub.com/authors/michelle-m-pillow

goodreads.com/Michelle_Pillow

amazon.com/author/michellepillow

youtube.com/michellepillow

pinterest.com/michellepillow

FEATURED TITLES FROM
MICHELLE M. PILLOW

<u>Magical Scottish Contemporary Romances</u>
Warlocks MacGregor
Love Potions

Spellbound

Stirring Up Trouble

Cauldrons and Confession

Spirits and Spells

Kisses and Curses

More Coming Soon

<u>Bestselling Paranormal Shifter Romances</u>
Dragon Lords Series
Barbarian Prince

Perfect Prince
Dark Prince
Warrior Prince
His Highness The Duke
The Stubborn Lord
The Reluctant Lord
The Impatient Lord
The Dragon's Queen

Lords of the Var Series
The Savage King
The Playful Prince
The Bound Prince
The Rogue Prince
The Pirate Prince

Captured by a Dragon-Shifter Series
Determined Prince
Rebellious Prince
Stranded with the Cajun
Hunted by the Dragon
Mischievous Prince
Headstrong Prince

www.MichellePillow.com

COMPLIMENTARY MATERIAL

WE THINK YOU'LL LOVE....

FOOLED AROUND AND SPELLED IN LOVE

BY MICHELLE M. PILLOW

A Happily Everlasting Series Novel

Welcome to Everlasting, Maine, where there's no such thing as normal.

Anna Crawford is well aware her town is filled with supernaturals, but she isn't exactly willing to embrace her paranormal gifts. Her aunt says she's a witch-in-denial. All Anna wants is to live a quiet "normal" life and run her business, Witch's Brew Coffee Shop and Bakery. But everything is about to be turned upside down the moment Jackson Argent walks into her life.

Jackson isn't sure why he agreed to come back to his boyhood home of Everlasting. It's like a spell was cast and he couldn't say no. Covering the Cranberry Festival isn't exactly the hard-hitting news this reporter is used to. But when a local death is ruled an accident, and the police aren't interested in investigating, he takes it upon himself to get to the bottom of the mystery. To do that, he'll need to enlist the help of the beautiful coffee shop owner.

It soon becomes apparent things are not what they seem and more than coffee is brewing in Everlasting.

CURSES AND CUPCAKES

BY MICHELLE M. PILLOW

A Happily Everlasting Series Novel

Welcome to Everlasting, Maine, where there's no such thing as normal.

Marcy Lewis is cursed (honestly and truly) which makes dating very interesting. With a string of loser boyfriends behind her, she's done looking for love in all the wrong places. That is until the new firefighter arrives in the sleepy seaside town of Everlasting. Nicholas Logan is unlike any other man she's ever had in her life. When someone starts sending her photographs that raise a red flag it soon becomes apparent that she's not just cursed, she's in serious danger.

Nicholas doesn't know what to make of the

charismatic young woman managing the local coffee shop. As a string of mysterious fires begin popping up around town, the two unite in search of clues as to who or what is responsible, discovering along the way that things are very rarely what they seem to be.

SPELLBOUND

BY MICHELLE M. PILLOW

Warlocks MacGregor Book 2

Contemporary Paranormal Scottish Warlocks

Let Sleeping Warlocks Lie...

Iain MacGregor knows how his warlock family feels about outsiders discovering the truth of their magical powers and shifter abilities: it's forbidden. That doesn't seem to stop him from having accidental magical discharges whenever Jane Turner is around. The woman has captured his attention, and, apparently, his magic and other "parts" don't seem to care what the rules are, or that the object of his affection might be his undoing.

Warning: Contains yummy, hot, mischievous MacGregor boys who may or may not be wearing clothing and who are almost certainly up to no good on their quest to find true love.

Warlocks MacGregor® 2: Spellbound Extended Excerpt

"*Dè tha thu ag iarraidh?*"

"What do I want?" Jane whispered, looking around in confusion for the speaker. She was unsure as to how she'd come to be outside. One moment she'd been in bed, the next in a garden. "I'm losing my mind."

She knew this garden. She'd itched to get her hands on it ever since she'd moved to Green Vallis, Wisconsin. The plants were choking from neglect, but beneath their twisted wildness was rich soil. Most of the trees and shrubs would be salvageable—if not at their current location, then transplanted elsewhere. The grounds were expansive and had so much potential. Being located on a hill above the small town, it had ample sunlight and natural drainage when it rained. It belonged to an old mansion that had just recently been purchased after decades of sitting empty. Everyone in town knew the story of its builder—the displaced English lord. He'd been a rake or a rogue or whatever they called the rambunctiously decadent men of the time.

Despite whatever the nobleman had lacked in his personal life, he'd had a great eye for creating picturesque beauty. The property came with eighty acres of land, including part of the surrounding forest with a stream running through it and the old English landscape garden. Yes, the giant house was nice, but Jane saw it more as a backdrop to the nature surrounding it. She couldn't imagine owning eighty acres of land. The mere idea of it was a kind of what-would-you-do-if-you-won-a-million-dollars pipe dream.

"Dè tha thu ag iarraidh!"

Jane flinched as she found the bearer of the mysterious voice. Why was a Scottish woman screaming at her? And why was the woman's tiny frame aging so rapidly Jane could see the wrinkles forming on the pretty face as if the woman was living an entire lifetime in a single afternoon?

Jane knew she was hallucinating. What else could this be? The doctors had warned her that her mind would eventually deteriorate. Even so, this hallucination felt very familiar as if she'd lived this moment but couldn't remember it.

"Thalla's cagainn bruis!"

"Chew a brush?" Jane tried to translate the woman's words. It made no logical sense that she understood any of it, as she didn't speak Gaelic.

She frowned, looking at an overgrown goose-berry bush a few feet from where she stood on the cobblestone path. Not knowing why she tried to obey, she lifted her arm in its direction but couldn't reach. Why couldn't she reach it?

She looked down. A light fog surrounded her legs. It held her immobile like metal shackles. Fog like shackles? She should be able to run through the fog.

"*Dè tha thu ag iarraidh?*"

"I don't know what I want," Jane answered, blinking rapidly as a wrinkled finger pointed a little too close to her nose. How could the finger be so close? The woman was nearly twelve feet away down the path near the mansion's exterior wall. Fear filled her, nearly choking the breath from her lungs. "Why can I understand what you're saying? Who are you? How did I get here? What do you want?" She remained rooted in place, like the wild overgrowth around her yearning to be saved. "I don't understand why you're yelling at me."

The aging woman's finger dissipated into mist but did not disappear. Instead, the mist surrounded Jane's head. She swatted it away, but the action only caused the mist to swirl up her nose. Around her, the plants moved, coming to animated life. They stretched and grew, aging like the now-old woman before her, then transforming into a beautiful combination of lilac and purple Scottish heather. The heady scent of flowers and honey was so strong it burned her nostrils and caused her eyes to water. Bagpipes sounded in the distance, impossibly carried on a wind that did not stir.

And then…nothingness.

To find out more about Michelle's books visit www.MichellePillow.com

Made in the USA
Middletown, DE
13 June 2019